THE ROOMMATE SITUATION

COLORADO SPRINGS UNIVERSITY
BOOK 1

FELICITY SNOW

Cover design by GetCovers

Formatting by Leslie Copeland

To anyone who feels a little different. Keep being you. Normal is boring.

ACKNOWLEDGMENTS

To my amazing beta readers, Hawthorne Gray, Donatella Coluzzi, Wren Vale, Sarra Lancey, and Amanda Martin. Thank you so much for all of your help and support on this story. And to my street team for spreading the word about Rory and Parker. I couldn't do this without you!

A special thank you as well to my amazing editors Jen Sharon and Becky Wenzel for making my work shine.

ONE

RORY

"I'm home!" I call as I close the door to the apartment I share with my boyfriend, and slide off my shoes. I'm feeling especially giddy today since it's my birthday and he promised that as soon as I got out of my last class we would celebrate. I'm in my third year of college at Colorado Springs University as an illustration major. Zach and I have been dating for almost eight months now, and living together for four, ever since the end of last semester. We spent almost the entire summer together, rather than me going home like I have the past couple of summers. I still saw my family, but it was a much shorter stay this time around because of Zach and I getting settled in our new place.

I run a hand through my unruly brown curls as I make my way down the hall and through the open living room and kitchen area, surprised that he hasn't come out to greet me when I know he's home.

"Zach?" I call, as I draw closer to our bedroom. "Baby?" We have a two bedroom apartment near campus, and use one room as the bedroom and the other one for a study room. My parents are helping with the cost of rent until I graduate and get a full time job. And because they know living in the dorms would be a challenge for me.

I hear loud moaning and cursing coming from the bedroom as I draw closer and frown. Is he jerking himself off right now? I'd assumed we'd be having sex later. Could he not wait? He's been home for what, an hour?

But as I reach the door I hear the tell tale slap of skin on skin and then a voice that isn't Zach's. "Yeah, fuck, harder."

What the hell? The door is wide open when I reach it, and my stomach bottoms out as my eyes widen and my face flames. My chest tightens and I can't fucking breathe. He's fucking another guy on our bed, in broad daylight, and he's not even trying to hide it.

Shit, I knew we were having problems but I didn't think he'd do this.

He turns and meets my gaze. I feel a sharp stab of pain when he smirks at me. He's not horrified he got caught, or ashamed or guilty. He's not telling me "It's not what it looks like" or any of the other lame excuses he could be throwing out there. It's like he fucking *wanted* me to find him with his cock buried in someone else.

"You fucking asshole," I snarl as tears fill my eyes and I hurry back the way I had come. He doesn't even bother coming after me as I slide my shoes back on and grab my backpack, heading out the door.

Happy fucking birthday to me.

I have tears still sliding down my cheeks as I sit at the campus coffee shop waiting for my friends Lucy and Jackson to arrive. I've been trying to drown my sorrows in a pumpkin spice latte, but apparently that only works as a pick me up when it comes to not doing as well as you would have liked on an exam, or your BFF not being able to hang out with you, but not so well when your boyfriend of eight months cheats on you.

My phone buzzes on the table and I turn it over, expecting it to be Lucy telling me she's delayed or something, because she always is, but it's a message from Mr. Asshole himself. And even though I know I should ignore it, at least until Lucy or Jackson gets here to play interference, I swipe and read. Big mistake, because I'm just crying harder and feeling more angry and confused than I was a minute ago when I read it.

Zach: Hey, look I'm sorry you had to see that, but it's not like you didn't see it coming.

Me: What the actual hell is that supposed to mean?

Zach: Come on, babe. A guy like you and a guy like me? You can't seriously expect me to not get some action on the side now and again. Especially when you haven't been available lately. I have needs.

What the fuck? Is he seriously making this out to be my fault? The fact that I'm actually doubting myself, wondering if I contributed to him cheating on me in some way, that maybe I am to blame, tells me this relationship was so much unhealthier than I realized. Shit. When it occurs to me that this may not be the first time he's cheated on me, I start to shake. How long has this been going on?

I turn the phone back over without responding and sigh in relief as I see Lucy approaching. There's music blasting through the speakers, and since the coffee shop is a part of the student center, which also houses a small dining hall, it's bustling with college students and profs trying to get their caffeine fix, grabbing dinner, chatting, and studying. Fortunately I have my earplugs in and it helps block out some of the noise.

"Hey," she says as she slides into the seat across from me. She has light brown skin and her black curly hair falls over her shoulders. She doesn't even have the word out before I'm a sobbing mess again and she's scooting over to my side of the table to sit next to me, pulling me to her and letting me rest my head on her shoulder as I cry. I don't care that we're in a crowded place where anyone could see me losing my shit.

"Hey, talk to me," she says, rubbing my arm with her hand and shushing me gently. When I finally croak out the words, she moves away, so stunned and clearly pissed off, that I almost fall over without her supporting me.

"Shit," I mumble, as I catch myself, then wipe more tears from my eyes.

"He did what?" she says, her green eyes stormy. "Hell, no. I'll go over there and castrate that bastard myself."

"Um, thanks," I say, "but I really just want to be here, with you guys right now, if that's okay. We can castrate later."

She purses her lips as if considering it, and then nods. She takes me into her arms again and I continue to cry.

"What the hell?" Jackson says as he joins us, sitting in the seat Lucy had previously occupied. He's tall and very thin with pale skin, and jet black hair. He wears dark eyeliner under his eyes and earrings and rings galore. He has a nose ring, and even a tongue ring. His eyes are a vivid blue and they widen when Lucy speaks.

"Zach is trash."

"Fuck," is all he says. Then looks at me. "I'm really sorry, babe."

I nod and sniffle. "Thank you. I just can't go back there. I mean, I have to eventually, to get my stuff, but not tonight. Not while he's there. I have to find a place to stay."

"You can crash on our couch," Jackson says, referring to the apartment he shares with two other guys.

"I know this is hard," Lucy says as she plays with my curls. "But I have to say, babe, I think you might be better off in the long run. I know you liked him, but Zach always kinda gave me ick vibes."

I stare at her, my eyes watery. "What? Really?" Seeing how he treated me tonight, I guess I shouldn't be surprised, but I never knew she felt that way.

She nods and shares a look with Jackson, telling me he agrees.

Jackson shrugs. "He wasn't mean or anything, at least not that I could tell, and I never thought he'd cheat, but yeah, Lucy's right, just bad vibes."

"Why didn't you guys say something, I don't know, months ago?" I say, irritation in my voice.

"Would you have listened? You were enamored with him from day one, and he seemed charming, I guess, but maybe that was the problem. He was a little too charming, you know what I mean?"

She's right. I've been infatuated with him since we met at a party about nine months ago. Honestly, I was surprised he noticed me. I'm typically the one in the corner with a book and headphones on because I can't handle how loud the music is, and my friends have dragged me along despite my desire to be alone, because they're convinced it's good for me to socialize. I don't mind parties sometimes, but I can't handle them for more than an hour and then I'm shutting down or getting overwhelmed by all the commotion and stimuli. My favorite way of socializing is just hanging out with the two of them. There's so much less pressure that way, and I'm horrible at small talk, so I go when they invite me and stay close to them until they're ready to mingle, and then I hide, or leave.

For whatever reason though, he managed to catch me in the short amount of time it took me to get a drink from the kitchen, and had flattered me endlessly. Told me how cute I was, how much he liked my glasses and freckles, and the way I dressed. Asked me where I'd gotten the bow-tie and suspenders I was wearing. Even told me how pretty my eyes were. I was so shocked that he'd deigned to pay attention to me at all, that when he suggested fucking in the bathroom down the hall I couldn't say no. He was not only insanely attractive, but he was the first guy to ever show a genuine interest in me, and I was lapping up the attention.

I've never been popular. High school was rough and I never had any sexual experiences at all until college. And even then it was minimal. I'm kinda nerdy and I've never considered myself particularly attractive. At five foot four I'm fairly short and skinny, and add social awkwardness to it, and it doesn't add up to much, so his attention felt like everything.

I had blown him, and then he had told me something had come up and he had to leave. I was disappointed he hadn't offered to reciprocate but shrugged it off. The next day he found me after one of my classes and it was the same thing, blowing him in the bathroom. Then he'd asked me to come to his place that night and we'd fucked for real.

It had been okay, but not anything memorable, and I had been a little discouraged that I had waited so long for sex only to have it not be everything I was expecting, but I figured it was just me, because he seemed to get a lot out of it. I just remember it hurting more than I thought it would, even for it being my first time, but when I mentioned it to him he told me it was normal and would feel better the more we did it. Spoiler alert, it did not.

My phone buzzes and I reach for it. I don't know what I'm expecting. Maybe for him to tell me he has a twin and the guy I saw fucking someone else in our bed wasn't him. Part of me really wants that to be the case because I still can't believe he cheated on me, on my fucking birthday.

Zach: Where are you? Come home. Let me make it up to you. I'll make you the birthday dinner I promised and we can talk. I'll even give you your present.

I just stare at it in disbelief before another text appears.

Zach: Come on, Rory, stop being so fucking childish and answer me. You know I didn't mean to hurt you, okay? We can work this out. I need you, baby. Don't do this to me.

Don't do this to him? As if he is somehow the victim here? More tears fill my eyes and slide down my cheeks. *No. No I don't fucking know you didn't mean to hurt me. In fact I'm pretty sure that's exactly what you meant to do or you wouldn't have left the goddamn door open and fucked him when you knew I would be coming home!*

The worst part is that I want to believe him so badly. I want to believe it was a mistake, that he didn't mean it, that somehow magically, he tripped and his dick fell in the guy's ass. Maybe Zach wasn't the boyfriend I'd always dreamed I'd have but he was mine, and it felt good to have someone who was mine, someone who wanted me. God, I know he's full of crap, but that doesn't stop me from considering going back and letting him "explain." Giving it another chance.

It's not lost on me that with all of these messages he's sending, never once has he apologized or even said he was wrong, or regrets what he did.

Zach: Seriously, come home, Rory. Come home. If you're off blabbing to your little friends I'm gonna be so pissed. You better not be saying anything to them. Just come home, and let's talk.

"Um, k, I think that's enough," Lucy says, sliding the phone out of my hands and locking it as I feel the blood draining from my face. "Can I make a suggestion?"

I nod and she takes my hand, giving it a squeeze that helps ground me.

"Leave your phone with me tonight. I won't look at it, I promise, but I don't think you should either. Nothing he has to say is going to be good and you need some time to clear your head."

I swallow and nod. I hate not having my phone on me, but she's right. It's not a good idea right now.

"What do you say to a movie night at my place?" Jackson says. "We can binge watch the *Avengers* movies and stuff our faces with junk food."

I nod, my tears having subsided and giving way to shivers. My brain is a foggy mess and I know it will take some time to process things. Lucy slides my phone in her bag and we make our way to Jackson's, Lucy with her arm around me the entire way.

I wake up the following morning with a smashing headache, hopping off the couch in Jackson's living room when my stomach lurches, and racing towards the bathroom.

As I'm vomiting up the food and the drinks from the previous night, everything comes back to me in a rush and I groan.

I jerk and put a hand to my head when I hear a bang on the front door. Slowly I make my way to my feet and flush, then rinse my mouth out before washing my hands. By the time I get to the living room, Jackson has already answered the door, and my eyes widen when I see Zach standing there.

"What the hell are you doing here?" Jackson says.

"Let me in, Jackson," Zach replies, sounding pissed. "I want to talk to him and I know he's here."

"I don't know what you're talking about," Jackson says, as I stand just out of sight of the doorway, listening.

"Look, I know I messed up," Zach says, his voice much gentler this time, and I find myself tearing up again. "I miss him. I need to see him. Please. Just tell him I'm here."

"I don't know what you're talking about," Jackson repeats. "If I see him I'll let him know you were here." Then he's shutting the door in Zach's face and turning around as Zach begins to pound on it again.

"Damn it, Jackson, let me in. I know he's here. He has to come home eventually. He can't avoid me forever."

It's quiet after that and I'm pretty sure he's gone, so I slink out from my hiding spot. "Thank you," I tell Jackson.

"Of course. Come on, let's eat breakfast. I need bacon and coffee."

I give a smile because that sounds pretty great.

"How are you doing?" he asks me, as we eat and sip on our drinks.

"I don't know," I say. "Pretty shitty, I guess."

"Makes sense. You know Luc and I are here for you. Whatever you need. You can stay here for as long as it takes you to find a place."

I nod, and take another sip of my coffee before saying, "I just can't help wondering if I pushed him to this. Maybe if I apologized, said I was sorry, maybe if I let him fuck me more often–"

"Oh, no," Jackson says. "We're not going there." I meet his gaze and he continues. "You are not responsible for this, Rory. No matter what problems you guys were having, you didn't make him cheat. Got it? I don't care if you were only fucking once every six months, if he had a problem with it he could have talked to you. He could have said it wasn't working for him because he needs to be with someone with a higher sex drive. He could have broken up with you. He didn't need to cheat."

I nod again, but I'm not convinced that's true, and I hate it. I want to believe Jackson but I have all of the things Zach has been telling me for months running through my head right now, along with those texts from last night. I know I can't go back to him, but I don't know how to not be with him, either. I haven't been single in a long time and he was my first.

As if reading my thoughts, Jackson says, "I know he was your first, and it's always hard when it's your first, Ror, but you deserve so much better than him. It hurts a lot right now, but you will be better off without him, and you'll find a guy who treats you the way you deserve to be treated."

I swallow when I realize something. "Shit, I should get tested." Tears fill my eyes yet again and I bury my face in my hands as my shoulders shake.

"You guys didn't use condoms?" Jackson asks.

I flush. "I mean, the first few months we did, but not after that. He got really insistent about going bareback, about how much better it would be. I didn't want to disappoint him."

Jackson sighs. "Hon, that's fine if that's what you want, but you should never feel like you are being coerced into unprotected sex. God, what an asshole. I'm starting to think more and more that he was a complete douche."

I start to sob again, so embarrassed by my own ignorance and stupidity, and inability to stand up for myself in a relationship where I should have felt completely safe doing so. I was just so scared of losing him, because I'd never had anyone pay attention to me the way he had, never had anyone desire me the way he had, that I let him say and do a lot of things I wasn't comfortable with.

"Hey," Jackson says, walking around the bar and sliding his arm over my shoulders. "You're gonna be okay. I'll go with you if you want me to. We can both get tested."

"Are you having unprotected sex?" I ask with a slight laugh.

"No, but it doesn't hurt to get tested now and again anyway."

I know he's just doing it to make me feel more at ease about the whole ordeal, but I nod anyway.

"Now, when would you like to go get your things?"

I sigh and wipe my eyes. "When he isn't there."

"Yes, that's a given, hon. Lucy and I will be going with you. You'll need help loading everything into your car."

It's not until I see Lucy later that afternoon that I get my phone back, and honestly I'm not even sure I want it. Not having it was kind of nice. I take it, but don't bother turning it on before sliding it in my pocket.

We make our way to the apartment and I use my key to get in, Jackson and Lucy following behind me. I know Zach's schedule well enough it wasn't too hard to find a time when he would be gone so we could get my things and be out of here before he gets back.

Even though I know I'm doing the right thing, it still hurts to be packing up my life and leaving the place I've shared with Zach for the last several months, the place I thought we'd be in together for a lot longer.

I leave the furniture and just take my clothes, toiletries, books, and other essentials. A lot of the dishes and cookware are mine so I snag those, including the silverware. I take my food from the pantry and the fridge and gather my meds. Once everything has been piled into my car, I drive it back to Jackson's, where most of it will stay until I find another place to live.

We head inside and have lunch before I have to get to my afternoon classes. I hug my friends and thank them for everything before dashing out the door.

My last class of the day is Visual Development, and by the time it's done and I've finished my shift at the campus bookstore, I'm exhausted. Fortunately I haven't run into Zach.

When I get back to Jackson's, Lucy is already there and they have food waiting for me. I seriously have the best friends in the world.

I turn my phone back on as I settle on the bar stool overlooking the kitchen, and my eyes almost bug out of my head when I see that I have twenty two missed texts from Zach. Mostly consisting of him saying he wants to talk and work things out, and the best part, that I'm overreacting. My eyes are stinging with tears and my face is hot as I finish reading the last few messages.

Zach: I know you were there today when I visited Jackson's

Zach: We need to talk, baby. You need me and you know it. Don't let a little misunderstanding get in the way of what we have.

Zach: That's how it's gonna be, huh? Well fuck you, Rory. Good luck finding someone else to put up with you, you little bitch. You know with how messed up you are you're lucky I ever gave you the time of day, let alone thought you were worth fucking. You can be someone else's problem now, if you can find anyone who will tolerate you.

Then there's an audio clip attached, and against my better judgment I click play, even as tears slide down my cheeks. The room is filled with the noise of two men grunting and panting, and the unmistakable sound of skin slapping skin. My face drains of color as both Jackson and Lucy stare at me, trying to figure out if they're hearing what they think they are, I'm sure, because I'm doing the same thing.

Yes, Zach sent me an audio clip of him fucking someone. I know I should turn it off but I can't bring myself to.

"You hear that, Rory?" he says, as the other guy moans louder in the background. "That's what a real man sounds like when he's getting fucked. That's someone who appreciates what I can give him. That's what you're missing out on, you selfish little bitch. This could be you. But you won't be getting my cock anymore. And I can promise you no one is going to want you besides me, Rory. Not the way you are in bed, with that pathetic little dick. No one is going to be as patient and as understanding as me. Remember that when another year has gone by and you're all alone, you miserable piece of—"

Lucy snatches the phone and ends the recording before it can finish, and I'm shaking and sobbing. I can't believe they just heard all of that.

"What the fuck?" Jackson snarls as Lucy wraps her arms around me. "Did he talk to you like that before?"

"I…" I don't know what to say though, the words are lost on my tongue and I just sniffle and cling to Lucy tighter. He's said some things that upset me, hurt me, but never with that level of disdain.

"Hey," Lucy says. "Don't listen to him, Rory, he's trying to get inside your head. He's a loser and an asshole and you're better off without him, that's for damn sure."

"Can I suggest that you block his number?" Jackson says. "He won't stop sending you those things, Rory, and you don't need that. It's making you so upset, babe."

"Yeah, I'll think about it," I tell him, sniffling again and wiping my eyes. He frowns, clearly wanting me to do it right this second, but he doesn't push me.

"Let's do something productive, like get online and see if we can find you a roommate," Lucy suggests. "It's fairly early in the semester so you should be able to find something near campus."

TWO

RORY

As I lie in bed that night, unable to sleep, I think back to when my parents had called me yesterday afternoon, just before walking in on Zach, and how I was telling them all about the plans we had and how I was looking forward to bringing him home with me for Thanksgiving this year. My parents and my little sisters are about a two hour drive away in Breckinridge, so I always make it back for the holidays and I had planned on introducing them to Zach, finally. I can't believe I have to tell them that not only is he not coming but that he fucking cheated on me.

Not yet, though. I'm not ready to say anything to them yet.

I remember when Zach asked me to move in with him. Well, insisted is probably more like it, though I didn't see it that way at the time. I was nervous, but I'll admit I was flattered, too, at how he seemed to be so attached to me. I wasn't sure if it was what I wanted or not but he convinced me, telling me we'd have more time alone together, that it would help our relationship. That he missed me and wished I was around more. I missed out on a summer with my parents and little sisters after not seeing them for almost two months because Zach was so insistent that I come back and help him get moved into the new place. Told me if I really cared about him and our relationship like he did I would put him first and stop being so selfish. That he needed me.

Now that I have the scenario running through my head again along with the current set of events, I'm realizing just how manipulative he was, making me feel like if I didn't do what he wanted and something happened between us, it was my fault, or like I wasn't a good boyfriend because I wasn't spending enough time with him. Conversation after conversation fills my head with all the things he's said to me over the past four months and how much he changed after we moved in together.

His charm evaporated and he became more easily irritated by me and my quirks. He didn't compliment me all the time anymore, he didn't bring me food when I was studying, he didn't text me to say how much he missed me. But I once again assumed it was just me expecting too much, and I didn't want to say anything and come across as too clingy. The one time I did mention his mood he snapped at me. Told me he was allowed to have bad days. The next morning he'd apologized and told me he'd just been tired, that maybe it would help if I didn't go to Lucy's and hang out that night, and we had time just the two of us. I ended up canceling plans with her to stay home with him. And he'd said some things while he was fucking me that night that had hurt my feelings so much I'd locked myself in the bathroom and cried afterwards.

It went on like that for months. Him telling me I was too high maintenance. Him criticizing me for something, generally something he had found endearing or at least tolerable before, only to have him tell me I was being too sensitive or too needy if I brought it up, or told him he had hurt me. He loved to remind me how much he put up with for me.

"Fuck," I say, as the memories bombard me. "I'm so

fucking stupid." I'm sobbing again as I realize just how miserable I've been the last several months, trying to be better and do better for him, keeping my feelings to myself so I didn't upset him, trying to be the good boyfriend who doesn't cause problems or get on anyone's nerves.

Then I remember what Lucy said after I heard that audio clip. *Don't listen to him, Rory, he's trying to get inside your head.*

But it's too late. He's already inside my head and he's so fucking loud I don't know how I'll ever get him out.

"Okay, it's time to get out," Jackson says a week later, setting his laptop aside and hopping off the bed. He makes his way over to his closet and flings the doors wide. "Come on, get dressed." He looks over to where I'm sitting at his desk, attempting to do homework.

"I really need to write this paper," I tell him.

"No, you really need to get laid," he replies. I groan. "Come on, Rory, you've done nothing but mope around for days, and you have been staring at the screen for twenty minutes. Your head's not in it, so let's take a break. You are getting some action tonight."

I bite my lip. "I don't know. I'm not sure I'm up for going out." Though at least my test results came back negative, so that's a relief.

He sighs and walks over to me, resting his hand on my shoulder. "I know you aren't big on parties and crowds, and I respect that, but you need to let loose a little, hon. See that life can still go on even if you aren't in a relationship. Have some fun. You've been so down, and you know what they say, the best way to get over someone is to get under someone else."

"I'm not exactly a catch, Jax," I say, and he narrows his eyes at me. "I don't know if you noticed this or not but Zach was my first everything. Guys weren't exactly knocking down my door before he came along."

"You did not just say that." He snaps his fingers from side to side. "Rory, baby, you are the cutest cutie to ever cute, you understand me? Just because Zach didn't know what he had in you doesn't mean every guy out there is a moron. Trust me, you are going to do just fine."

I can't help the small smile that forms on my face.

"You good?" he asks. I nod. "Fabulous, we'll only stay for an hour or so, and if you aren't feeling it we'll head home, okay?"

"Okay."

"Now, where are those jeans that make your ass look positively biteable?" He winks and I flush as he digs through my clothes. "Text Lucy and tell her to meet us at *Raves* in thirty minutes."

When we walk out the door twenty minutes later I'm freshly showered and dressed in my ass biting jeans and a blue button up with a red bow tie and gray suspenders.

When we reach the club I slide earplugs in my ears that block out the background noise, but still make it possible to hear the people around me. It helps me not get so overwhelmed by everything.

Lucy meets us outside and we walk into the club together. I see the colorful lights flashing over the dance floor and the sweaty bodies moving to the beat. The smell of alcohol and lemon fills the air as we make our way to a booth in the back. Lucy and I sit while Jackson gets us drinks.

Honestly, as much as I am not huge on crowds, this is nice, getting out with my friends, and I do enjoy dancing.

We finish our first round of drinks and then Lucy grabs both my and Jackson's hands and pulls us out into the throng of people on the dance floor. I sway my hips and raise my arms as I move to the music, surprised at how much I'm enjoying myself.

"Hey," Jackson says, moving closer to me as Lucy grinds up against a pretty girl nearby, both of them smiling, "looks like those jeans are doing the trick. I told you you wouldn't have any trouble."

I blink, and he motions with his chin towards the bar. When I turn my jaw nearly drops. There's no way that gorgeous guy is staring at me. He must be at least six foot two, with short dark hair and a body that tells me he definitely works out. He blushes and gives me a sexy smile, and a wave that's insanely cute, and I feel my cheeks heating. I bite my lip to keep from grinning from ear to ear as I wave back. Is this real?

"Hey, what's the matter?" Jackson asks when my smile disappears in an instant, replaced with a racing heart and sweat gathering on the back of my neck that has nothing to do with the lights and multitude of bodies around me. *You know with how messed up you are you're lucky I ever gave you the time of day, let alone thought you were worth fucking. No one else is going to want you, Rory. You had it so good with me and you don't even know it.*

I shake my head. "I can't. He's so hot. There's no way he wants me. I can't do this. Zach was right. I don't know why I'm here."

"Hey," Jackson grips my shoulders and turns me to face him. "Zach wasn't right about a damn thing. That guy wouldn't be staring at you if he wasn't interested. You're not picking out curtains. It's just a fuck, to get that asshole off your mind. Don't let him ruin it." He grips my chin and takes a deep breath and lets it out, and I follow.

"Good?" he asks. I'm still nervous, but I nod. I need to do this. I want to do this. God, he really is hot. Those broad shoulders and thick chest. Arms with muscles for days. The narrow waist and thick thighs.

I can't help doubting myself again, though, as I make my way over to the gorgeous guy, dressed in snug fit jeans and a white T-shirt that clings to his upper body, showing off said physique. There's no way he was really looking at me, right? Maybe the guy behind me? Maybe at Jackson? My best friend is insanely pretty. It was probably him and I am making an idiot out of myself.

God I shouldn't be doing this. But it was me he was waving at and it's definitely me he's looking at now.

I haven't had sex in two weeks and that's enough to make even me horny, and apparently more bold than usual, because I am not the type to approach gorgeous men in clubs. But maybe a mind blowing orgasm will help get me out of my funk and provide me with enough clarity that I can write my fucking paper.

I'm not interested in being fucked. It's something I did for Zach because he liked it but I just never enjoyed it very much. Blow jobs, though, I love those, both giving and receiving, and the thought of having this guy's dick in my mouth is making my mouth water and my cock twitch.

But why me? Out of all the guys in here, whom I am sure he could have his pick of, he was looking at me? The shrimpy little nerd? It doesn't make sense.

"Hi," I say, stopping in front of him.

He beams at me. "Hey, cutie. I like your bow-tie." His voice is vibrant and cheerful, and not really what I expected, but I find myself liking it. "Suspenders, too."

God it's like Zach all over again, the way he started flattering me endlessly. And look how well that turned out. But I'm not dating the guy, just getting off with him, hopefully. "Yeah, um, listen, I don't mean to be rude but I'm incredibly horny and I just broke up with my boyfriend and just need to unwind, if you're cool with that."

He grins at me. "Man, you don't mess around, do you, little dude?"

I flush, both at his words and the nickname. Little dude? Honestly, I've never been this bold before but if I don't grab the bull by the horns so to speak, I'm afraid I'll chicken out, and I really am horny.

He grabs my hand and pulls me around the corner and into the bathroom, not letting go until we're in the furthest stall from the door. He closes and locks it before turning back to me, and God, I want to climb him like a tree. Those muscles are something else, and his hazel eyes are heated when they lock on mine, like he really wants this. Wants me. I don't understand it but I would be foolish to analyze it too much.

"Can I kiss you?" he asks, his breathing picking up, and I notice the bulge in his tight jeans. God, he's big. I lick my lips and nod, and not a second later his lips are on mine. I have to stand on my tiptoes to kiss him, but fuck, it's worth it. His hands are so big they pretty much engulf my entire face as his warm, chapped lips slide over mine. I open for him the moment his tongue slides along my lower lip. God, he's a good kisser. I don't think Zach ever kissed me like this. He tastes like potato chips and lime and it's addicting.

He presses me against the wall and I gasp when I feel his rock hard cock against my stomach. He smells like toasted marshmallows and vanilla and it makes my cock twitch. "Can I blow you?" he asks, pulling away, his pupils blown wide. My heart pounds a little harder. I've always been a bit self conscious about the size of my dick. It's a little on the small side at only four and half inches, and Zach never failed to point that out, which just made it worse, but I want this. I need it, so hopefully if this guy is disappointed he'll keep it to himself.

"Yes," I reply, and he grins. Then he's kissing me again and I have to hold back a whimper as his large fingers skate through my curls. God, this is unlike anything I've ever felt before. Why is it so different with him? So much better?

I almost whimper again when his mouth leaves mine and then laugh a little when he looks at my suspenders like he isn't sure what to do with them. "These are adorable, but how do we get them off?" he asks.

I reach over and slide one of the straps off my shoulder, then the other, letting them fall to my sides. He flushes. "Oh, right. Thought I had to unhook them from your pants or something."

I grip his face and pull him back to me, smiling, because he's just too damn cute. I love that he's so flustered he couldn't figure out how to undress me. He lets me kiss him a few more times before he pulls away and sinks to his knees. Oh, God. My heart rate picks up again and sweat gathers on the back of my neck as he unzips my pants. I want this, I know I do, and he looks incredible on his knees in front of me. *Fuck, if I'd wanted to hear my partner whining like a bitch when I fuck them I'd have gone to bed with a girl. You a fucking girl, Rory?*

Don't let him in your head, I tell myself. *Don't let him ruin this.*

My pants fall to the floor and then he's gripping my jock-strap and pulling it over my erection, letting it spring free. Precum is leaking out already, and he slides his tongue over the tip, lapping it up and moaning. It's so fucking hot it makes my cock twitch. "Shit," I whisper. His gaze meets mine and those hazel eyes are partially hooded, he looks so blissed out.

"God, you're pretty," he says, and I almost gasp, because it sounds so sincere, and I've never had a hookup, or even Zach, tell me that before. Zach told me I was cute on occasion, at the very beginning of our relationship. My friends call me cute, but it's the first time someone has used the word "pretty" to describe me, and I kind of like it. Okay, I really like it.

My cock twitches again and he grips it in one of his huge hands and laps at the tip over and over until I'm biting my lip and trying to keep from squirming or whimpering. "Fuck," I mutter, when he licks from the base to the tip and then swallows me down. "God, that's good." He hums around me, making pleasure shoot straight to my balls. Then he's gripping them in his other hand and rolling them, tugging gently as he takes me to the back of his throat. "Shit," I gasp, unable to stop myself. God, his mouth is wicked. He bobs up and down on me for a few more seconds, then takes me to the back of his throat again, and I combust, biting my tongue to keep from crying out as my cock spurts load after load into his warm, wet mouth. I stare down at him as he swallows every last drop, then pops off of me and presses a kiss to my tip, before his eyes meet mine.

"Thank you," are the words that come out of my mouth next, and then my cheeks heat as I groan at how stupid that was. What is wrong with me?

He smirks and chuckles a little. "You're welcome, freckles."

Okay, that's a new one. I'm not sure what's with the nicknames but I find myself liking them. He reaches up and adjusts my glasses on my nose so they aren't sliding off, and I flush. "Can I?" I ask, even though my heart is still racing and my anxiety is picking up again.

He pulls my pants back up with him as he stands and tucks me back into my jock strap. "Sure can," he says, grinning at me.

I lower myself to my knees in front of him and pop the button on his jeans. His erection is straining against his zipper and I see the large wet spot on his black boxer briefs when I tug his pants down. Wow, he's even bigger than I thought. And I can't get enough of that toasted marshmallow and vanilla scent. I find myself burying my nose in his groin and inhaling, flushing when I feel his big paw on my head, gripping my curls.

"Damn, freckles," he breathes as some of his precum slides across my cheek.

Don't be such a fucking whore, Rory. It's embarrassing. Just suck.

I pull back and take the head of his cock in my mouth, sucking and licking around it. I want to moan at the feel and taste of him on my tongue, but I don't. His grip on my hair loosens and I take him a little further.

You know with how messed up you are you're lucky I ever gave you the time of day, let alone thought you were worth fucking. You can be someone else's problem now, if you can find anyone who will tolerate you.

I take him deeper as tears sting my eyes, and it's not from his size, or how full I feel with him inside me. I suck harder and he hisses, but I don't let up.

It's a good thing you have two holes cuz one of them is pretty useless, isn't it?

More tears fall down my cheeks as my head bobs up and down on his cock.

A guy like you and a guy like me? You can't seriously expect me to not get some action on the side now and again.

I gasp as I slide off of him and push myself to my feet. Tears are sliding down my cheeks and I don't say a word before I'm unlocking the door and bolting from the bathroom.

THREE

RORY

"Shhh," Lucy coos as I sob on her shoulder yet again. When I got out of the bathroom at the bar I rushed over to Jackson and he pulled me aside immediately when he saw how upset I was. We left with me barricading myself behind my two best friends so that the hottie I'd left mid blow job wouldn't see me.

"I don't know what's wrong with me," I sob. "I can't get Zach out of my head and it's ruining everything. God that was so embarrassing. He was so hot, and so sweet, and I am such a fuck up."

"Okay," Jackson says, sitting next to me. "We aren't going to talk like that, babe. You had a bad moment, you'll come back from it." He pets my hair and I sniffle. "Have you blocked him yet?"

I shake my head. "No, but I stopped reading his messages."

"Honey, you need to get rid of him," Jackson states. "In every sense of the word. That boy is no good."

"It's not just the text messages, though," I say. "It's things he said while we were together that are making me so anxious and upset I can't even give a fucking blow job."

"God, he really did a number on you, didn't he?" Lucy says. "I'm sorry we didn't notice how awful he was sooner. I mean, I never liked him for you but I didn't realize it was this bad."

I shake my head. "It's not your fault. I didn't say anything. And he was a different person in public. There's no way you could have known. It's taken all of this for me to realize just how much he hurt me."

"It might take some time, but you've got us," Jackson says. "You'll find yourself again, and realize how amazing you are. Maybe pushing you to hook up was a bad idea."

I wipe my tears. "No, I wanted it." I sigh. "It was a nice little confidence boost until I blew it, or didn't, I guess."

Lucy snorts and Jackson chuckles, and then we're all laughing. "God, he was so hot, too," I groan.

"Yeah, he was," Jackson agrees. "Look on the bright side, though, you'll probably never see him again."

My phone pings then with an alert, and when I pick it up I see that my ad for a roommate has a reply. I suck in a breath. It's been up for a week and I hadn't heard from anyone and was beginning to lose hope. God, whoever it is I hope they're not a partier, or a slob, but I'm not sure I have much choice in the matter.

"What's it say?" Lucy asks, reading over my shoulder.

"He's a student. His roommate decided to move in with his girlfriend, and he's looking for someone else to share in the cost of rent. Utilities included. No smoking or drugs. No pets. Only a few blocks from campus." I glance at them. "Should I reply?"

They nod and I start typing and hit send. I get a reply almost instantly, telling me I can come by and look at the place as soon as I want and ask him any questions. Honestly, I don't much care what it looks like, as long as he's not a creep and I won't be fearing for my life.

We set up a time for tomorrow afternoon for me to meet my potential roommate and see the apartment. If everything seems to be on the up and up, I'll move my things in the same day, since it's all sitting in my car anyway.

I let out a deep breath. Maybe this new roommate situation will help me get my mind off of Zach, and the hot guy from tonight.

"Okay, let's do this," Jackson says. He came along with me to check out the apartment and help me move my things in, assuming everything goes well enough. It's in a decent area, lots of college students, and I can take the college bus or drive to my classes, or ride my bike. I could even walk when the weather is nice enough, which it should be for a few more weeks, at least until October rolls around and it starts to get chillier.

We make our way inside the building and up the stairs to the third floor. "3D," I say, looking around, and Jackson points when he sees it. We stop in front of the door and I knock, begging for the guy inside to not be a creeper, or a serial killer, or a republican.

"Just a second," I hear on the other side of the door and my eyes widen.

"We have to go," I say in a hushed voice to Jackson, grabbing his arm and tugging.

"What? Why?" But by then it's too late and the door has swung open to reveal my hot hookup from last night. His eyes widen when he sees me, and then to my surprise a huge grin breaks out across his face. I don't miss the oven mitts on his hands and the pink apron with white lace around the edge. Not gonna lie, I wasn't expecting that.

I hear a snort from Jackson and my cheeks heat.

"Hey, freckles," the guy exclaims. "No way! You're the one looking for a roomie?"

"Uh…" I stammer, trying to figure out a way out of this.

"Yes, indeed," Jackson says, shoving me forward and making me almost slam into Hot Guy's very firm chest. He steps back enough that I manage to brush against him instead, but still stumble, and he has to grab me to keep me from face planting.

"Woah, you okay?" Hot Guy asks, his arms wrapped around me, pressing me to him and his apron, which is covered in flour and what smells like cake batter. Wow, it's actually really nice, and I have to force myself to pull away when he steadies me.

I glare at Jackson but he just winks at me and saunters inside, making himself right at home as he looks around. I sigh and follow him.

The kitchen is off to the right. There's a decent sized living area with a futon and a large sofa in a floral print that looks like a garage sale find, but is still in decent shape. Across from the sofa is a large flat screen tv. There's a room just beyond the living area and the door is shut.

It smells amazing in here. Like cinnamon and vanilla, and my stomach growls.

Hot Guy closes the front door and turns to us. "You two go ahead and look around," he calls as he moves into the kitchen. "I'm gonna check on the cupcakes. You let me know if you have any questions."

I catch up to Jackson down the hall as he's peeking into the bathroom and smack his arm. "I can't stay here," I hiss. "I'll have to stay in my room the entire time because I'm too humiliated to look him in the face."

"Babe, this is a great place, and he's a total sweetheart, I can tell."

I narrow my eyes, even though I'm pretty sure he's right, but I was dumb enough to date Zach for eight months because I thought the same about him, so what do I know? "How can you tell?"

"Vibes, babe," he says, then fucking pats the top of my

head. "And cupcakes? The guy bakes cupcakes. And that apron? Seriously. He's like the hunky version of Martha Stewart."

"Hey, he could have human remains in those cupcakes for all we know," I retort, and Jackson smirks.

"Babe, I know this is a little awkward, but I really think it's going to be fine. Maybe it will even give you a chance to explain what happened last night?"

I frown. "I can't tell him I chickened out because my emotionally abusive ex got in my head."

"Why not? Then at least he knows it wasn't him."

I sigh. "I'll think about it."

"Good boy," Jackson says, patting me again. I shove his arm away and he laughs, then saunters the rest of the way down the hall. He stops at what I'm assuming would be my room, assuming also that the room with the closed door is Hot Guy's.

It's got a dresser already, a bed frame and mattress with nothing on it, and a closet. It's bright and cheerful, in an off white color. Not really big but big enough, with a large window on the opposite wall.

"Okay, time to get your things, huh?" I nod, even though I'm still mortified about living with the guy who I ran away from last night in tears. I follow Jackson back out to the combined kitchen, living area where Hot Guy is taking cupcakes out of the oven and setting them on the stove. He turns to us and grins, sliding his oven mitts off.

"They're a little hot but you guys are welcome to have one when they cool down. You'll want to wait for the frosting, though. That's the best part."

I nod but don't say anything.

"Any questions? It's a decent place. Good neighbors. And you'll have privacy. You've got your own bathroom, and I'm not picky about what's on the tv so you can watch whatever you want. And I promise I'm not a druggie or anything. You saw everything except my room and the attached bathroom. I can show you if you want but it's pretty messy."

"No, that's okay," I tell him. I do notice the main living area is pretty clean, which I appreciate, though I don't know if he did that just for my visit or if it's always like this. Guess I'll find out. I tend to get stressed in a space that is super messy so if it gets bad I may just have to stay in my room. Zach was good about keeping the place clean for the first couple of months but complained about it after that, told me I was OCD and needed to get a life, and that he had better things to do with his time, so I stopped saying anything and would just clean it myself or stay away.

Fuck, why did I not realize what a jerk he was until now? I just assumed he was right, and that I was the problem one in the relationship. Too picky, too needy, too high maintenance.

"I can help bring your things in if you want?" he offers, and Jackson nudges me. When I look at him while Hot Guy is removing his apron he makes the shape of a heart with his hands and I roll my eyes.

"I'm Parker, by the way," Hot Guy says, and reaches out to shake Jackson's hand and then mine. "Parker Hayes."

"Rory," I squeak out, and my cheeks flush as I try not to squirm. God, this is so awkward. Out of all the guys I could be rooming with it has to be him. He grins at me again and it makes me feel a tiny bit less awful.

With all three of us working it doesn't take too long to get my things in my room, and when Jackson pulls me into a hug after Parker has returned to the kitchen, I grip him tightly. "Don't leave me," I whisper. "I could end up in the next batch of cupcakes."

He chuckles and pulls back, planting a kiss on the top of my head. "You're going to be fine, babe. I'll call tomorrow and see how you're doing. See you later, okay?"

I nod and hear Parker offering Jackson a cupcake to go. I groan and sit down on my unmade bed, but then start when I hear a knock, and look up.

"Sorry, little dude," he says, and I see he has a cupcake on a small plate. "I thought you might like to have one. They're good. I promise."

"Thanks, but I'm not hungry," I lie. His face falls but he recovers so quickly I barely notice it, and my chest squeezes.

"Oh, uh, I think this is yours," he says, reaching in his pocket and pulling out something. He steps forward and shows it to me, resting on his palm. It's one of my earplugs and I didn't realize it was even missing until I got back to Jackson's last night. He found it and kept it, in the off chance he would run into me?

"Thank you," I murmur, glancing at him and taking it.

"Well, I'll let you get unpacked," he says. "Unless you want some help? I don't mind."

I swallow but shake my head. "No, thank you."

He nods again and scurries off, and I fall back on my bed with a sigh. God, I feel like such a jerk. But there's no way I can have him in here helping me after last night. It's not him. I want to tell him that so badly but I'm so embarrassed and he doesn't need to know about my whole life story just because we're roommates. I don't need to be dumping that on him.

I feel a tear sliding down my cheek and wipe it away. I'm tempted to call Jackson and tell him he needs to come back and get me, but I know that's not going to work. Somehow or other I'm going to have to make the best of this situation.

FOUR

RORY

A couple of hours later I'm almost completely unpacked, including the sheets and comforter for the twin sized bed and getting my toiletries in the bathroom down the hall. I haven't heard or seen Parker since he left my room, but when I make my way out to the kitchen to grab a chair so I can hang my curtains, I see him sitting on the couch in the living room with a book in one hand and an apple in the other. He takes a huge bite, and I flinch when I hear him crunching loudly.

As I reach for the chair I second guess myself and turn to him instead. Maybe I should extend an olive branch. "Hey, you busy?" I ask, and he looks up at me so fast I wonder if he was waiting for me to talk to him.

"Nope. You need something?" God, he's so eager it's kind of adorable.

"I uh," I clear my throat as he sits on the edge of the sofa, his book and apple discarded on the coffee table as he stares at me, waiting. Jesus, if he was a dog his tail would be wagging and his tongue would be sticking out. "I could use some help getting the curtains up in my room. I can't reach."

His eyes light up as he stands. "You got it, little dude." He claps me on the shoulder and heads down the hall. The rod was already up. I just need to get the curtains on it and put it back up.

He spies the navy blue curtains on the bed and gestures. "This them?"

I nod, hands in my pockets. He takes the rod off without even stretching and my dick twitches when I get a really nice view of both his strong back and his tight ass. Jesus, how does he eat all those cupcakes and stay in the kind of shape he's in?

I'm hating myself for not finishing that blow job. His cock was delicious and felt so good in my mouth. Damn Zach.

I hold one end of the rod and slide a curtain on while he does the same to the other end, then we reattach the knobs at the end, before he slides it back in the slots above the window.

"It's looking good in here," he says, his gaze darting around the small room.

"Thank you," I say, flushing.

"You hungry? I've got dinner in the oven." His eyes are sparkling and I can't believe how excited he is about the idea of something so simple as eating a meal with me. I can't believe he wants to be around me at all after I left him with blue balls.

"Uh, I'll grab something for myself, but thanks, anyway," I tell him. He looks so sad I want to cry but I quickly add, "Thanks for helping me with the curtains. I hate heights, so not having to stand on a chair was really nice."

He beams. "No problem, freckles. Anytime you need something just let me know."

He heads back out to the kitchen, and I follow. I'm tempted to barricade myself in my room for the foreseeable future, but I know I can't. If he's going to be my roommate I'm gonna have to get comfortable around him.

I don't have much of my own food yet, so I remind myself

I need to go shopping in the morning. For now I'll survive on instant rice and a banana.

My stomach growls when Parker pulls the pan out of the oven and sets in on top of the stove. There's chicken in it that's dripping with what looks like three different types of cheese and covered in breadcrumbs with parsley sprinkled on top. Damn, it smells amazing.

"You sure you don't want any?" he asks as he watches my instant rice heat up in the microwave. "There's more than enough."

I give a small smile. "Can't," I say, "I'm allergic to good food."

His eyes widen. "Really?"

I chuckle. "I mean, yeah, sort of. I have to stay away from certain foods, and one of them is dairy. Kinda sucks, actually."

He blinks at me with those big hazel eyes. "You can't have dairy?" He seems so upset on my behalf it's almost comical.

I shake my head.

"Dude, that's just sad. I can't imagine my life without ice cream, or milk, or cheese or chocolate. Oh, god, I'm getting depressed just thinking about it."

"Yeah, I'm not a huge fan, but it is what it is." I take my instant rice out of the microwave and dump it into a bowl as he dishes the chicken onto his plate along with some broccoli that is also drenched in cheese. We eat standing for a bit before he speaks again.

"Wait, is that why you didn't want a cupcake?"

I nod and he lets out a breath. "That's a relief. I thought…" He bites his lip.

"What?" I ask when he runs his fingers through his dark hair, showing off his bulging bicep in the process and making my dick twitch again. For fuck's sake. Even if last night did end horribly, my body still knows what it wants, apparently. Those hands on me again. Those arms around me. Those lips on mine. God, my lips are tingling again just at the memory of how he kissed me.

"I thought maybe I'd done or said something to make you uncomfortable."

Now it's my turn to blink. "Like what?"

He shrugs. "I don't know, I was just worried about you after you ran off crying last night, and then you were pretty nervous when you got here and saw who I was. You really didn't want your friend to leave. You seemed so upset and I hated to think I'd caused it somehow or that you wouldn't be happy here."

Fuck. My chest squeezes at how insanely sweet he is. I left him in the middle of a blow job and he was worried about me? Instead of being pissed? Shit, Jackson was right. I should tell him what happened so he knows he isn't to blame. "No, it wasn't you. I promise. I was…I just…I was so embarrassed after running off like I did at the club and then there you were, and I didn't know how to not be mortified."

"You sure?" he says. "I was worried about you."

"God, that's really sweet," I say. "And no, I promise, you didn't do anything wrong. I, uh, I just got out of a bad relationship, like I told you last night and I guess I just wasn't as ready as I thought I was to jump back into the hookup game."

He nods and we eat. "You have other food you have to stay away from?" he asks.

I nod as I swallow my rice. "Gluten and eggs."

His eyes widen. "Jeesh, what's left if you get rid of all of that?"

I chuckle. "Not much. I'll get more food tomorrow and then I can cook for myself. I won't always look this pitiful." I give a small smile and he smiles back. God, he's cute.

"I don't mind cooking for both of us," he says, surprising me. "I mean, unless you want to cook."

"I fucking hate it," I tell him. "I do it because I have to, but I definitely don't enjoy it. But you don't have to do that. It's a pain to find recipes that I can eat, and you probably won't like them." Zach complained all the time about my diet being too restrictive, as if he was the one who had to limit or avoid certain things altogether or he'd be sick in the bathroom all night. I remember him coming home and heating up the food I'd made, only to toss it in the trash with a comment about how disgusting it was and how he didn't know how I could eat like that, like I had a choice. It pissed me off that he wasted my food, too. I didn't mind him having some if he was actually going to eat it, but taking two bites and then tossing it irked me. I wasn't made of money and he didn't seem to care that he had just tossed the food I was planning to eat for lunch or dinner the next day, only to sit down with a bowl of cereal instead.

He'd always complain about my food but never wanted to be bothered to cook for himself, unless we had friends over and then he'd insist on it because no one would want to eat "the garbage I made."

"Why did you say you weren't hungry instead of telling me the truth? About your allergies, I mean?"

I swallow and blink. "Oh, um, I guess it's just easier than explaining everything. It gets tiring explaining a medical condition to every person I meet, and a lot of people don't understand, so I don't bother."

He shrugs. "I get that. It would be frustrating, and they might not understand, but it's still good for them to be educated. Lots of people have food sensitivities or allergies. I think people need to be more aware of how much food affects their bodies. A lot of people feel sick all the time, or tired, or sluggish, or irritable, and don't even consider it might be what they're eating."

I blink again. "Yeah, you're right. I got diagnosed with a gluten sensitivity when I was a kid, but it took longer for the other ones to show up."

"What happened?"

"I started having stomach pain, and trouble swallowing when I was thirteen or so, and after a bunch of tests that didn't detect anything they decided to do an endoscopy. Turns out my esophagus was narrowed and inflamed due to something called eosinophilic esophagitis. I was on meds for a while but they weren't enough so we had to go pretty drastic with the diet."

"Man, you've been on this diet since you were thirteen?"

"I cheat sometimes, but it never ends well."

"Well, I'm gonna find some amazing meals for you to eat that taste good and keep you out of the bathroom."

I flush because I can't believe we've gone from exchanging blow jobs one night to talking about my stomach problems the next. But it's not nearly as weird and awkward as I would expect it to be. Parker is really sweet, and thoughtful. Though I wonder how long that will last before he realizes how frustrating it is to live with me.

When I wake up the next morning it's to the smell of bacon and waffles, and it's delicious. I stumble out of bed and slide my glasses on, before making my way down the hall and to the kitchen, where my eyes go wide at the sight of Parker in nothing but a towel.

"Oh, hey, you're up," he says, voice as cheerful as ever. "I made breakfast." He glances over at me and his eyes widen. Then he's in front of me and gripping my face in his hands. "Are you okay? Did you get hurt?"

I blink, trying to focus on his question and not the fact that he's practically naked, his gorgeous muscled chest inches from my face, and that he smells amazing. His big hands gripping my cheeks brings back memories of our hook up and I'm flushing instantly. "Um, no," I say. "I'm fine." *Except that I want to fucking climb you like a tree.*

"What happened to your nose?"

I blink again. "My–" Oh, the nasal strip. I reach up and touch the clear band aid-looking apparatus across my nose. "I have allergies. It helps me sleep at night without being congested." I pull it off easily and wiggle my nose, and he sighs in relief. Then I'm standing there speechless when he presses a kiss to the tip of my nose.

"That's good," he says, walking back over to the stove. "You scared me, little rabbit."

Little rabbit? I think that's my favorite one so far. I put the nasal strip in the trash and then grab some coffee, before sitting down at the table. I try to keep from staring at his ass, but it doesn't work very well.

"So what are you allergic to?" he asks as he dishes some bacon onto a plate and sets it down in front of me. I snatch a piece up and take a bite. "Oh, everything," I say. "Trees, grass, mold, dust, you name it."

"Wow, that's rough. You try allergy shots? My mom did those for a while and they seemed to help a lot with her allergies."

"Uh, no, I don't handle needles very well," I say, just the thought making me nauseous.

"Oh, yeah, that would make it harder, huh?" He gives me a grin as he sets a waffle down in front of me with syrup, and my dairy free butter. Then he's back with fresh fruit and dairy free whipped topping.

"I didn't buy that," I tell him. He flushes.

"I did. This morning. There's a King Soopers just down the way. I also picked up some gluten free flour and almond milk."

My cheeks heat. "You did all that for me?"

He shrugs. "It's no big deal. I wanted waffles and I wanted you to be able to eat them. They're gluten, dairy and egg free."

Wow, I think I might cry. "I'll pay you back for the food. You shouldn't have to spend your money on things that are for me."

He shakes his head. "Nope, I wanted to do it, and I'll use

it, too. Now eat up. I'm gonna go get dressed. I have class soon."

I gobble down the waffles and fruit, then snatch another piece of bacon, before making my way to the bathroom to shower.

Once I'm dressed in my usual pants, dress shirt and this time a lime green bow tie and suspenders, I head to my morning classes, then my afternoon shift at the bookstore. It's fairly slow so I'm able to get some reading done for one of my classes while I'm there. When my phone buzzes in my pocket I take it out, and can't help the smile that crosses my face when I see a text from Parker.

Parker: hey, take a look at this and let me know if it sounds good for dinner. Then there's a link that I click on and it takes me to a website where I see a gluten and dairy free lasagna. I can't believe this guy is researching meals for me and offering to do the cooking because I told him I hate it. Damn, my heart is fluttering.

Me: it looks great, but I'm buying the ingredients this time. I'll head to the store after I'm finished with work. Probably be home around 7ish?

Parker: you got it, little rabbit! See you then. Smiley face emoji

I'm about to reply with my own emoji when I hear an all too familiar voice and look up to see Zach standing there with his arm around some guy, a wicked grin on his face.

"Hey, Rory, how's it going?" he says. "You haven't been responding to my texts so I thought I would drop by. This is Chad, by the way. He's the guy I was fucking when you walked in on us." My cheeks flame and it only gets worse when he leans closer and says, in a voice that is intentionally not a whisper, "I fucked him every night this week, and he took it so well, Rory. He didn't complain that I was too rough. And he didn't sound like a bitch in heat, either. I came in him so fucking hard every single time. God he milked my cock so well. Better than your ass ever could."

My cheeks are so warm I must look like a tomato and I have to keep the tears from stinging at the corners of my eyes. What has he been telling everyone about me? What has he told Chad about me?

To add insult to injury he leans over the counter and knocks into my coffee cup, making it topple and spill all over the counter and my book, even getting some on my pants as he says, "Oops, so clumsy," and cackles along with Chad as they stroll away.

I do my best to wipe up the mess, but it takes more time than I would like since I have to run to the nearest bathroom for paper towels. I have tears sliding down my cheeks as I dry off my book, but when I try to separate the pages they tear like tissue paper. Fuck. This wasn't a cheap book, either, and now I'll have to buy a new one, and I hate asking Mom and Dad for more money. They aren't poor by any means but they're already doing so much for me. Plus I can't say Zach ruined it. I still haven't told them what happened.

"Hey, freckles, I didn't know you worked here," I hear and look up to see Parker standing there as I wipe my pants off, concern written all over his face. "What happened?"

"My ex happened," I tell him, sniffling. "He's a real sweetheart."

"Really? Sounds kind of like an asshole to me," he replies and I look up at him, his face completely stoic. Is he for real?

"No, he is," I say. "I was being facetious."

His mouth opens in an "O" and I can't help smiling a little at the image of a lightbulb going off over his head. "Right, yeah, that makes sense. You okay?"

"I will be," I tell him, though Zach's words are still running on repeat through my head and I can't get rid of the sick feeling in my stomach.

"Anything I can do?"

"No," I sigh, "but thanks for asking. I'm just gonna finish up here and then go home to change before I head to the store."

"Can I get you to ring this up for me?" he asks, and I realize he is holding a pair of sweats with the school's name on it. Right, of course he came in here for a reason.

"Yeah, sorry," I say. "Just let me wash my hands really quick?" He nods and I scurry off. When I get back he's waiting for me, and I ring his purchase up before he waves goodbye and heads out the door.

FIVE

RORY

When I get home later that evening I change out of my sticky clothes as quickly as I can and shower for the second time that day. The coffee smell is all over me and has leaked through my pants, and I'm dying to get into fresh clothes.

When I come back out to the living room, I see Parker on the sofa in the sweats he bought earlier and no shirt. He's got his laptop out and is typing away, his legs splayed across the sofa and a bag of potato chips nearby on the coffee table. I stare at those gorgeous pecs and tight abs for far too long before I say, "I'm headed out. Be back soon."

"Oh, hey, you want me to come with you? It'll go faster." He sets his laptop aside and wipes his hands on his sweats.

"Sure," I say with a smile, happy for the company. It'll help distract me from the shit that happened earlier, and I have decided I like spending time with Parker.

He scurries to his room, and I can't help letting out a sigh when he returns with a T-shirt now covering his beautiful, smooth chest. "You good?" he asks.

"Yeah," I reply, and grab my keys. I have to laugh when we reach my car and he has to slide the passenger seat back several inches before he can even get in. His head nearly touches the top and he looks like a giant. "Sorry," I say, and he just grins at me.

"No worries, I'm used to it."

When we reach the store I grab a cart and Parker snatches a basket. We split up, agreeing to meet back at the registers in twenty minutes. I'm there first, and when I see him coming my way, my anxiety spikes. He's surrounded by three other well built guys similar in size to him, though not quite as bulky, and they're laughing like they're having the best time, and I'm all of the sudden feeling very out of place and awkward.

"There he is!" Parker calls when he sees me, and waves, then gestures for his friends to follow. I swallow as they get closer. "This is my awesome roomie, Rory," he tells them, beaming at me.

My anxiety fades in an instant at how excited he is to introduce me to his friends. Me. Nerdy, awkward, me. "Hi," I say, giving the three guys a wave.

"This is Preston, Blake, and Chris," Parker says, gesturing to each of the guys in turn and they wave at me. "They're in some of my phys ed classes with me."

Preston is a couple inches shorter than Parker, with striking blue eyes and a baseball cap on over his blond hair. Lots of muscle but more of a swimmer's build. He's gorgeous and has several tattoos decorating his arms.

Blake and Chris aren't bad looking either. Blake is the shortest but still significantly taller than me, with dark hair that's pulled back in a messy bun and tan skin. Chris is the tallest next to Parker. He has chocolate colored skin and warm brown eyes and his dark hair is even shorter than Parker's.

"Nice to meet you," I say.

"Same," the one named Chris replies. "You've got a good roommate here." He claps Parker on the shoulder and Parker blushes. "He was my roommate freshman year."

"We gotta get home," Parker tells them. "You guys coming over on Sunday to watch the game?"

They nod. "Sweet," Parker says, and then proceeds to give each one of them fist bumps before they say goodbye and then make their way back down the aisles.

"They're cool guys," he tells me and I nod. "You don't mind them coming over, do you?"

I'm not crazy about the idea because it will probably be pretty loud, but I'll just put my earplugs in and do my best to block out the noise. I don't want to tell him not to invite them when he's so excited, and I don't want to be the annoying roommate.

We make it home and unpack the groceries, and then Parker starts cooking. It smells decent once it's been in the oven for a bit, so hopefully it tastes okay too.

"What happened to the cupcakes?" I ask, realizing that they're all gone.

"Oh, uh, I gave them away to the neighbors. I couldn't eat twenty four cupcakes."

"Why did you make them, then?"

"I bake when I'm nervous," he tells me with a flush, and I blink.

"You were nervous yesterday? About meeting me?"

His flush deepens and he runs his large hand through his hair again. "Yeah, I mean, I really wanted you to like it here, and I wanted you to stay. I've always been pretty extroverted and I grew up with five brothers and sisters, so I really don't like being alone. I mean, just having another person in the apartment makes a difference even if we're not hanging out, and I hated the idea of having to find someone else. My old roommate had only been gone for two days and I was lonely." He glances away. "That probably sounds ridiculous."

"No, it doesn't. I mean, I like being alone, but not for days at a time, and I know not everyone is like me. It makes sense. I'm sorry if I made it worse for you by being a buttface."

He laughs. "Nah, I'm just glad you're here." He ruffles my

hair and we sit down to eat. The lasagna isn't delicious but it's good, and I am thankful that I didn't have to make it, so I offer to do the cleanup instead. He sits at the bar while I do and after knowing how much he hates being alone, I don't mind.

"You're a phys ed major?" I ask, and he nods.

"Yeah, I want to be a P.E. teacher, or maybe a coach someday, or both. I really like working with kids and I like sports and fitness, so…" He shrugs.

"Yeah, I can tell," I say, then flush when he grins at me.

"What about you? What's your major?"

"Illustration. I would love to illustrate children's books at some point."

"That's awesome." His eyes light up. "Do you have a specialty?"

I can't help smiling. Zach never really gave a shit about my major, or asked me questions about it. In fact he tried to talk me out of it. "I really enjoy watercolors. Acrylic paint is nice, too."

"Do you have anything I can see?" he asks, and I smile wider at how eager he is.

"Yeah, just a second." I finish loading the dishes in the dishwasher and wash my hands, then grab my phone out of my pocket and find some of the pictures I took of my recent work and show him the screen. "These are pictures of ballerinas I painted for my little sisters for their birthday, and then if you swipe you'll see the one I did of my parents for their anniversary a few months back."

"Wow, these are amazing," he tells me. "Damn, little rabbit, you got skills."

I beam. "Thank you. I enjoy it, too. It helps me unwind." Zach always thought I was decent at art, but he was constantly trying to convince me to switch majors, saying being an illustrator wasn't very practical and you had to be really good at it to succeed. Well, I knew I had room for improvement, but I also knew I was good. They wouldn't have let me in the program here if I wasn't, and hearing it from Parker means a lot.

He nods and hands the phone back. "You have twin sisters?"

"Yeah, Ava and Addison. They were my parents' "oops" babies, but I love them."

"How old are they?"

"Seven. So much energy."

He laughs. "You said you had *five* brothers and sisters?" I ask, unable to keep the shock out of my voice. Parker grins.

"Yeah, I'm the middle child. Two older brothers and three younger sisters. My brothers, Aaron and Archer are twins. They graduated college last year and live together now, near my parents. My sisters, Amy, Jessica, and Hope are ten, fourteen, and eighteen. It's a full house when we're all home."

He's smiling widely and I can tell how much he loves his family. "It sounds like you're all really close."

"Yeah, we are. They're out in California so I don't see them a lot, just holidays and summer break, but I love going home."

"And they know you're gay?" I ask, my face flushing when I realize maybe I shouldn't have asked that, but he just grins wider.

"Practically threw me a parade when I told them," he says with a laugh, and I smile. "And both my parents are bi."

"Really? They just told you that?"

He shrugs. "We grew up knowing, yeah. They wanted to make it clear that even though they were in a relationship with each other, there were other ways for love and families to exist, so they told us from the get go about both of them being attracted to men and women, but finding each other and falling in love. And they didn't want us to ever be afraid of who we were attracted to."

"I really like that. And your siblings? Are they straight?"

"Archer is pan, Aaron is straight. Hope is bi. I'm not sure about the other two. I think they're still figuring it out."

I finish wiping down the counters and putting away the leftover food, and then I join Parker in the living room, him on the couch and me on the chair as we do homework.

I can't remember a time where I felt this content.

PARKER

Gosh, I can't believe Freckles is my roommate. How lucky could a guy get? I never even thought he would give me a second look that night at the club, and when he did, damn, I was on cloud nine. He's so stinking pretty, and he doesn't even realize what he does to me. Those curls, the freckles scattered over his nose and cheeks, his blue framed glasses, his goddamn bowties, everything about him is just adorable. Especially the way his nose twitches when he's nervous or agitated, and the way it scrunches up when he's concentrating on something, like right now while he works on his homework.

He reminds me of a bunny rabbit, hence the nickname. I can't seem to stop using them with him, and he doesn't seem to mind.

I was so scared when I thought I had upset him, but knowing what I know now, about his jerk of an ex, God I just want to throw a cupcake at the fart face for upsetting Rory. And I want to make sure that whatever he dealt with with him, he knows he's safe here, with me. And that I will always respect him, because he deserves it. He deserves to be treated like the amazing dude he is.

Would I love to get another chance at having him suck my dick? Absolutely. Up until he bolted and I freaked the fuck out it was incredible. He's got a mouth like a fucking hoover. But I'm also realizing just how much I want to be his friend, and how much I'm enjoying getting to know him. So if he wants more at some point, I definitely won't say no, but I won't bring it up, either.

I glance at him as he sits with his legs crossed on the chair. He's so small he fits perfectly just like that. My dick twitches when I remember how amazing it felt to kiss him, and have my hands in his soft curls.

He looks up at me and gives me a soft smile. "Everything okay?" he asks.

I smile and nod, and go back to my homework.

SIX

RORY

"So, how's the new roommate sitch?" Lucy asks as she, Jackson and I Facetime that night. I'm sitting on my bed, holding the phone in front of me and I can't stop smiling. The way Lucy's grinning I know Jackson told her who my roommate is.

"It's good," I say.

"You guys boning?" she teases.

"No, we're not. God, not that I don't want to, though. He's so hot, and honestly, incredibly sweet, too. I don't think I'm ready for that, though. Not after the other night." Lucy and Jackson still don't know about all the hurtful things Zach said to me when we were having sex, and just how much it affected me. He would complain that I wasn't in the mood enough, but he demeaned me so much when we did fuck, that I got self conscious and didn't want to have sex nearly as much after that. That just made him even more irritated. I felt like I was always having to be someone else in bed with him, and he was so in control I was just there for him, to help him get off. It was never about the two of us, and it certainly was never about me. I want to be with someone who cherishes me, who worships me, who makes me feel safe.

"It's too bad I'm a lesbian or I'd be all over that," she says, and I glare at her.

"Don't you touch my Parker," I say, and she and Jackson both laugh.

"Your Parker, huh?" Jackson says. "I think our little Rory has a crush on his roomie."

I flush. "Shut up. I have to go. You two are awful."

They laugh again and I grin, then say goodnight, and it's not until I'm lying in bed a while later, starting to doze off, that I realize I enjoyed myself so much this evening, I forgot all about Zach being a jerk to me earlier in the bookstore.

It's Sunday, and Parker and I have been roommates for a week now. Honestly I've enjoyed it so much I find myself missing him when I don't see him for an entire day because our schedules don't line up. We have some evenings together and a few mornings, but most of the time we either don't see each other at all or we're running past each other as the other is coming in or out of the apartment. He has been doing pretty much all the cooking, while I do the cleanup, and it's amazing. He's found multiple recipes that he actually enjoys and that I can eat, too. And he's even watched a couple of documentaries with me and enjoyed them. One was on Lucille Ball, whom I absolutely love, and Parker found it fascinating. He'd never even heard of her, which I was blown away by. The other was on serial killers, which may have been a mistake as neither one of us slept that night, it turns out. And after realizing it, we decided that if we ever can't sleep again we'll see if the other is awake too.

Part of me is tempted to watch another creepy documentary just so I have an excuse to climb into Parker's bed and cuddle. Being wrapped up in those strong arms would be amazing, and I bet I would sleep like a baby.

Right now, though, I'm in my bedroom, trying not to lose my mind as he and his buddies hoot and holler at the tv, commenting on whatever ball game they are watching. I don't know anything about sports, except that they are loud and I suck at them. The real problem, though, is that between the tv being at full volume, (or at least it feels like it is), and their voices carrying through the apartment, I'm about to either throw up, or cry, even with my earplugs in.

I did okay for the first hour, but it's been two hours now and my brain feels like it's going to explode. I've got a headache and I'm feeling so overwhelmed I'm starting to shake. My brain is a foggy mess and I couldn't work on homework if I wanted to, which I don't. I could go to the library but I'm exhausted and I honestly just want to relax at home in my pjs and watch tv or read for a bit before going to bed.

I hate this. I hate that I can't be normal and just deal with it, but I've never been able to handle settings like this for long without getting overstimulated. Noise is not my friend. I even have to barricade myself in my room after a couple of hours at home with my little sisters, or leave the house all together and go somewhere quiet so I can get a break, because no matter how much I love them, they're so rambunctious. Mom and Dad realized it pretty early on and they take them out when I need some quiet time if they can. But I hate inconveniencing other people when they're just living.

I groan and roll over on my bed with my hands over my ears, just praying it will be over soon, and a second later there's a tap on my shoulder. I start and roll over.

"Hey, freckles," Parker says as I scramble off the bed. He eyes me, then the bed, and I sigh when I remember that my lights are also dimmed to help me shut out some of the stimuli, as well as my curtains being drawn. Not totally weird because it is dark out, but I can tell he knows something is up.

"You okay?" he asks. "Are you trying to sleep?" He looks at me, still fully dressed. "We haven't seen you in a while. The guys are wondering where you are."

"I just don't feel really well," I tell him. There's a loud shout from down the hall and I can't help flinching.

Parker raises an eyebrow. "Are we being too loud? Is that why you're in here?" he looks around, "like this?"

I shake my head, even as it throbs, wrapping my arms around myself as I shiver. I feel lightheaded and my skin prickles, like tiny little needles all over my body.

"Hey, you okay?" he says, more worry in his voice now as he steps closer and grips my shoulders. I can't help whimpering and covering my ears when another shout echoes down the hall.

"I'll be right back," he tells me, then bolts out of the room. Shit, I've ruined everything. His friends are going to hate me. He's going to hate me. I'm such a fuck up. I climb back in bed and pull the blankets up over my head as tears slide down my cheeks.

A second later I feel a tap on my shoulder and turn to see Parker standing there with a glass of water. I blink and sit up, wiping my tears away. I take the drink and the Advil he hands me and swallow them down.

"They're gone," he says, tapping his ear, and I remove the earplugs, only then realizing that the noise is nonexistent now.

"Where did they go?" I ask. "What about the game?"

"I asked them to leave. I couldn't let them stay knowing how upset you were." I shiver for a whole new reason when he strokes his fingers through my hair, and I have to keep myself from melting against that big, broad chest.

"I'm sorry," I mumble as another tear escapes. My breath hitches when he swipes it away with his thumb.

"Don't apologize, little dude," he says. "You should be able to feel comfortable in your own home. I just wish you would have said something. You looked miserable."

"I didn't want to cause problems," I tell him.

"Why not? Your needs matter, too. I know we can get loud. We can watch the games somewhere else from now on."

"Your friends must hate me," I mumble, and he chuckles.

"Nah, they could never. They're cool. Just don't suffer in silence next time, okay? I don't like upsetting you."

I nod. "Thank you." I'm expecting him to leave, but my eyes widen when he makes himself comfortable on my bed, his back against the pillow that he's propped up, then crosses those big, muscular legs and pats his lap.

"Lay down," he says. I do, not really knowing why other than the idea of resting my head in Parker's lap is very appealing, and when I've got my legs stretched out in front of me and his scent surrounding me, I begin to relax. I almost fucking purr when his soft strong fingers start to massage my scalp, my eyes closing on instinct. "This okay?" he asks.

I nod. "Yeah, it feels amazing." His fingers are on both sides of my head, rubbing, stroking, moving to my temples, and behind my ears, and God, every muscle in my body liquifies as I moan. I can't fucking help it.

He chuckles and I flush. The pad of his thumb moves over the center of my scalp and tension oozes out of me as a shiver races down my spine.

"Fuck." I'm so relaxed I might fall asleep. I open my eyes and realize my dick is starting to tent my sweats, and I don't even care. I look up at him and grin lazily. My shaking has disappeared, the tingles dancing across my skin are gone, and my head feels infinitely clearer. I think the Advil is starting to kick in, too.

"Better?" he says with a chuckle. I nod. He leans over then and presses a kiss to my forehead. God, I want those full, chapped lips on mine again, but before I can even think about more, he's lifting me up and sliding out from under me.

"I'm gonna get you an ice pack and then I think we should head to bed." He leaves and I sigh. When he returns, I take the ice pack and then slide under the blankets and slip my kitty kat sleep mask over my head before lying down. I want so badly to ask him to stay, to sleep in my bed with me, to cuddle, but I can't, because my bed is tiny and because I don't want to be too needy. So I say goodnight and he shuts the door behind him.

PARKER

Fuck, I swear I try to fall asleep, but I'm so damn horny from touching Rory and having him purring like a kitten in my lap, and letting out the sweetest little moans and whimpers, watching his cute little dick twitching and perking up as I ran my fingers through his hair, I can't get my own dick to calm down. I genuinely just wanted to help him after seeing him so out of sorts, but apparently my body didn't get the memo. It's like everything is amped up times a billion when I get close to him. Leaving was the hardest thing, but I was going to be very hard, very soon if I didn't, and I didn't want to make him uncomfortable. My dick would have been pressed against his head.

Crab nuggets. Why is he so fucking cute? I don't know, but I've been lying here with a raging hard on for over an hour and I can't do it anymore. I slide my hand into my boxers and let out a breath when I come in contact with my very hard dick. It's been leaking like crazy and I have a sizable wet spot. I use my precum and slick myself up, moaning as my hand moves up and down my shaft. I spread my legs and grip myself harder, biting my lip as I picture Rory's adorable face, his button nose, and those wild curls. My breathing picks up and I reach down to tug on my balls, making my back arch. "Fuck," I gasp. God that feels good, and fantasizing about my roomie has me aching to come. I remember what it was like to have his dick in my mouth that night at the club, the way he gripped my hair, the way his pert little ass felt in my hands when I gripped it as he thrust into me. The taste of him exploding on my tongue.

I bite my lip harder as I let out a stifled groan and spray all over my hand, soaking my boxers in my release.

Damn, little rabbit, look what you do to me.

SEVEN

RORY

Another week has gone by and I'm in the art studio working on a painting for one of my classes, enjoying the silence and breathing in the scent of chalk, citrus and turpentine, when my phone buzzes in my pocket. I set my brush and palette aside and wipe my hands on my apron before pulling it out of my back pocket.

Jackson: So Lucy and I want to know when we're going to be invited over to hang at your new place and get better acquainted with Mr. Gorgeous McSweetie pants

Me: You can come anytime you want. You know that. Except right now. I'm not home.

Jackson: Yes, we know. We've been standing outside your apartment for five minutes.

Me: Omg! Why?

Jackson: Oh, wait, I see him. He's coming up the stairs. We'll just hang with him until you get here. Smile emoji. Kissy face emoji. Devil emoji.

Me: I'll be there in fifteen minutes! Be nice!

Jackson: No rush. Winky face emoji

Oh, boy. I finish up as quickly as I can and hang up my

apron. I have dried paint on my fingers and on my shoe, and probably on my face, too, but I don't care. I scurry out of the studio as quickly as I can and practically run home, flinging the door open when I get inside.

"Hey, I'm here!" I call, out of breath, only to be greeted by the sound of laughter from the next room. I set down my bag and kick off my shoes before making my way into the living area, where Jackson and Lucy are sitting around the coffee table with Parker, laughing over something I missed, heaps of junk food spread out in front of them. I can't help smiling, because they've only been here for a few minutes but they look like they've never been more at ease with each other.

"Hey! Freckles!" Parker cheers when he sees me, and I flush as my two best friends exchange looks, and Jackson turns to me and mouths *freckles.* "Come sit and join us. Your friends are awesome, by the way."

"Yeah, I know," I say, taking a spot next to him on the floor.

Jackson winks at me and I flush again.

After talking and goofing off for a bit, Parker suggests a game of pictionary. Jackson and Lucy groan.

"What's wrong?" Parker asks.

"Rory is an art major. Whoever has him on their team will win. I can't draw worth shit," Lucy says.

"It's true," Jackson affirms, and Lucy slaps him.

"Ooh, I get freckles," Parker says, shooting his hand into the air, and I flush. "You ready to kick some behind, little dude?"

"Okay, what the hell," Jackson grumbles playfully, and I bring out a large sketch pad and easel from my room.

We use the ever trusty internet to find things to draw, and I go first. Parker starts shooting off random words as soon as my marker hits the paper and they're not even close. I'm laughing so hard I can barely keep drawing and Jackson and Lucy are cackling, too. Parker just keeps going, so enthusiastic he's about to jump out of his seat. I'm so excited when he finally jumps up and shouts, "Jellyfish!" about two seconds before the timer goes off, I shriek and throw myself at him.

"Yes!" I say, my arms wrapping around his thick neck and my legs locking around his waist. He doesn't even budge under the onslaught and it takes me a second to realize what I've done when he stares at me, flushing and grinning, his big arms wrapped around me.

"Sorry," I mumble, sliding off of him and clearing my throat. "Your turn." I hand the marker to Jackson and he gives me a knowing smirk before sashaying towards the easel.

Parker and I win the game by a landslide but Jackson and Lucy are super cool about it, laughing at how badly they are doing. Parker actually isn't terrible at drawing like they are so it was kind of an unfair game, but I'm okay with that. We all had fun, and that's what matters.

"Girl, you know that boy is a catch, right?" Jackson whispers as he and Lucy are saying goodbye at the door that night.

"And so are you," Lucy adds with a smile.

"I know," I tell them, "I mean, I know he is, and I'm starting to believe that maybe I am, too." I look back at Parker as he wipes down the coffee table. "I don't know if I trust myself yet, to find someone who won't treat me like Zach did, you know? I don't want to be wrong again."

Lucy steps forward and gives me a hug. "There's no rush," she says, pulling away, then glances down before meeting my eyes again.

"We wanted to apologize for not saying something to you earlier about Zach. Even if we thought you would be dismissive or anything else, we owed it to you to at least give you all of the information, and let you make the choice, and we dropped the ball. I'm really sorry, Rory."

"We're really sorry," Jackson chimes in.

"Thank you," I say. I had already forgiven them, but it's nice to hear anyway.

Lucy smiles. "But he has serious heart eyes for you, babe. And remember what I said about Zach having a bad vibe?"

I nod, and her smile widens. "None of that here," she says.

I smile back and wave goodbye, shutting the door when they've disappeared.

PARKER

It's a couple of weeks later when I arrive home after my afternoon classes and a group project that took way too long, that I find Rory sitting at the kitchen bar, staring at his phone, ashen faced as he bites his thumbnail.

"Hey, little rabbit," I say, setting my backpack and keys aside and moving towards him. "What's going on? You don't look so good."

"Hmmm?" he says, looking up at me, blinking those big blue eyes. He's dressed in a pair of leggings and an oversized sweater now that it's October in Colorado, and he looks absolutely scrumptious. His sleeves are so long they swallow his hands, but I love it. He looks so bite sized and I want to fucking nibble on him.

"You okay?" I say.

He swallows and sets his phone down, wrapping his arms around himself. "Yeah, I," he takes a deep breath in and lets it out. "I just got an email from my doctor, my gastroenterologist actually, and they want me to get some blood work done before my next procedure." He shivers and I open my mouth to ask what's the matter with that when I remember.

"And you don't like needles." He looks at me and shakes his head. "Damn, I'm sorry, freckles. That sucks."

"Yeah." He bites his lip and glances at me, but then looks away again, like he was about to ask me something and then changed his mind.

"You wouldn't want some company, would you?" I ask,

and he turns to me, his eyes filled with hope. "I mean, I wouldn't mind if-"

"Yes," he squeaks, then flushes and covers his mouth, with his hand still covered by his sweater sleeve, and I can't help laughing.

"No problem," I say, nudging his arm. Apparently the nudge was more like a shove because he yelps and flails as he slides off the bar stool, and I reach out to grab him when he starts to tip over, gripping the edge of the counter with one hand and my arm with the other. Oops. "Sorry."

"All good," he says, steadying himself and letting out a breath. He shoves his glasses back up on his nose. "I'm scheduling the appointment for the day after tomorrow, if that works. Early morning, because I have to be fasting and I can't eat until I get it done."

"Yeah, that's fine," I say. "Just let me know when we need to be there and I can drive."

"Thank you," he says, giving me one of those adorable as hell smiles.

I fix us dinner while Rory sits at the counter working on a drawing for one of his classes, and then we eat together.

Afterwards, I sit on the sofa while he cleans, and I smile when I hear him humming *You Need to Calm Down* by Taylor Swift as he works. I look up to see him swaying his hips and moving his head back and forth, and I'm brought back to the night I met him once again, seeing him on that dance floor and being so completely captivated by him.

My chest squeezes at the same time that my dick twitches, and of course that's the same time he chooses to look up and smile at me. Fucking fudge cake, he's making me all gooey inside and I don't know what to do about it. I've never felt so drawn to someone before, never felt so protective over them. But that smile and the way he's dancing also tells me he's doing a little bit better than he was a couple of weeks ago. He's gotten more confident and comfortable in the time that he's been living here, and that makes me happy.

He goes back to his project at the bar after that, and I pop my headphones on so I can listen to music without disturbing him while he works. It's about an hour later when I finally finish my homework for my *Physical Education for Children* class. I stand and stretch and then head to the bathroom. When I get back out, Rory is gone.

I'm kinda bummed because I was hoping to actually hang out with him a little bit tonight before bed, but oh well. I sit on the couch and turn on the tv, and a minute later I hear his padded feet coming down the hall and around the corner. I can't help smiling when I see him in polka dot pajama bottoms and an oversized T-shirt. On his nose is one of his nasal strips. I've gotten used to them by now and don't bat an eyelash when he wears them.

"Hey, little dude, thought you went to bed."

"Not tired yet," he says, and then to my surprise, settles in right next to me on the sofa instead of taking his usual place on the chair, his knees bent and his feet tucked up underneath him. We're close enough that we're almost touching, and I don't know if that's good or bad because now I just want to reach over and put my arm around him, or hold his hand.

"Another documentary?" I ask and he nods with a grin.

"If that's okay?"

"Of course." I hand him the remote so he can choose. I really don't care what we watch as long as I get to be close to him. I notice that as we're watching the nature documentary he's inching closer and closer to me. Eventually he sighs and rests his head on my shoulder, and a shiver runs down my spine.

"This okay?" he asks, and it's so timid and hopeful my chest squeezes even as my heart is racing.

"Yeah," I croak out. He smiles and turns back to the screen, and I have to will my dick not to react to his proximity. Damn, he smells good, too. Like pumpkin spice and nutmeg. It makes me want to bake something with pumpkin in it. Later though. I'm not moving as long as he's here.

About twenty minutes later I hear him snoring softly, and even though I could poke him or shake him awake, I don't. Instead I scoop him into my arms and carry him down the hall, his head resting against my chest.

I have the hardest time ever setting him down in his own bed, my arms and chest aching with the loss, like Rory is meant to be there, being held by me.

"Night, little rabbit," I whisper, and turn off the light, closing the door behind me.

EIGHT

PARKER

Two days later, we're heading out the door to Rory's appointment. He's putting on a brave face but I can tell he's anxious. He's slightly pale and he keeps biting his nails and taking deep breaths in and out.

"Who went with you before?" I ask him as we make the short drive, me behind the wheel.

"Oh, um, Zach went with me once, but he said it was embarrassing for him so I never asked him to go again."

My jaw clenches. "He what?" I don't get angry easily, but hearing these stories about his ex makes my blood boil.

Rory nibbles his fingernail, looking at me, then shrugs.

"That is messed up, little rabbit," I tell him.

"Yeah, I'm realizing that." He gives a small smile. "I'm starting to be more and more thankful every day that he cheated on me, because if I spent another year with him, or even another month, I might have actually gone my whole life believing it was okay for him to treat me like that."

"Why did you let him treat you like that?" I ask. He wraps his arms around himself as he answers.

"He was my first. I had never really had another guy

show interest in me before him, and I just didn't realize how messed up some of the things he said and did were. When I first met him he was charming and funny, and did kind things for me. It wasn't until we moved in together that he started to change. And I think, part of me just didn't want to believe it. I mean, my parents are great. They've always supported me, so it's not like I was seeking out a toxic relationship or anything, I just never had someone fawn over me the way he did at first. But the longer we were together, and the more we spent time alone, the worse it got. And I realized he never really cared about me."

"I'm sorry you didn't get a better first experience, little rabbit."

"Me too," he says, a sad smile on his adorable face.

"Well, you have me now, and even if you puke your brains out or pass out, I promise I won't be embarrassed."

"Thank you," he says.

When I pull into the Quest Diagnostics parking lot I turn the car off and wait. "You ready?"

"No," he tells me. "But better get it over with."

As we near the building Rory keeps playing with the sleeves of his jacket. Underneath is a short sleeve button up and bow tie. This one is black, with suspenders to match, and he has red skinny jeans on his legs that look amazing on him, showing off his little bubble butt.

I only hesitate for another second before I reach over and take his hand in mine, giving it a reassuring squeeze, and I hear the slight gasp that leaves his lips, but he doesn't pull away. Instead he squeezes my hand back and we walk inside that way. I stay holding his hand as we sit and wait for his name to be called. His leg is bouncing and he's biting his thumb nail, but I think I'm still helping him stay grounded a bit. He relaxes even more when I rub my thumb over his hand, and I hear a soft sigh as his leg ceases its movements.

I even get so bold as to press a kiss to his curls. We get a few looks from the other people waiting their turns, and I'm sure they're judging us for something, but I don't give a shit.

"Rory," they call after a few more minutes, and he stands, still clinging to my hand.

"You want me to go back with you?" I ask, and he nods, so I follow. While he's giving them his paperwork and paying, I sit beside him in the extra chair. He's literally doing everything with one hand so he doesn't have to let go of me, and I'm finding it really sweet, but also my chest squeezes with how nervous he must be.

"You're being really brave," I tell him softly.

"No, I'm not," he mumbles. "People do this all the time. It shouldn't be such a big deal."

"But it is a big deal, to you. It's scary. But you're still here. That's brave. Everyone is brave in their own way."

"This your boyfriend?" the lady behind the desk asks, a fond smile on her face. She has dark skin and her hair is pulled back in a ponytail as she types.

"No," Rory says. "Just a friend." He looks at me. "A really good friend."

My cheeks heat. "Aww, little rabbit," I say, and nudge him. He flushes, then and I realize what I called him, but he doesn't seem bothered by it, just flustered.

"You nervous?" she asks, and Rory nods.

"Don't like needles," he says.

"Oh, yeah, that's rough. If you tell them ahead of time they can have you lie down. That might help."

He gives a small smile and nods.

"Okay, we've got you all checked in," the lady says. "You can have a seat around the corner. They'll be calling you back shortly."

Rory nods and we stand, making our way to a second waiting area. "You got this, little dude," I tell him, as he grips my hand like a vice.

Fortunately it's only a couple more minutes before they call Rory back, because he needs to get this over and done with or he's gonna work himself into a tizzy. He doesn't let go of my hand as he follows the phlebotomist back to a sectioned off room. There's a chair and a table like you would see in a doctor's office. On the counter are several different containers with vials in them, each with different colors on the top.

I don't want to overstep, so I wait for Rory to say something. When the woman taking his blood asks him to sit he clears his throat and says, "Um, actually, could I lie down? I don't handle needles very well and if I'm not lying down there's a good chance I will pass out." He looks embarrassed but I am so stinkin' proud of him for speaking up and advocating for himself.

"Oh, of course, hon," the lady says. "We'll do our best to make you as comfortable as possible."

He tugs me over to the table and climbs up on it before removing his jacket and handing it to me. Then I take his right hand again as the phlebotomist steps towards him and wraps the tourniquet around his upper arm on the left side.

"Do you know which arm is better for this?" she asks, tapping the crease of his elbow and having him make a fist.

"I don't think it matters," he says. I can tell his voice is shaking slightly but he's doing so well.

The woman gives him a warm smile. "I think I found a really good one. Go ahead and lay down, sweetie." He does, his head resting near mine. I scoot a little so I don't have to reach so far to keep hold of his hand.

"Do I need to move?" I ask, worried I'm in her way. I don't want to make it harder for her and thereby harder for Rory.

"No, you're fine," she says. I see her prepping the needle and then moving back by Rory's side.

"Just a little poke," she says. Rory closes his eyes and takes a deep breath in, his body tensing up when she inserts the needle, his eyes closing tightly as he squeezes my hand.

"You're doing amazing, hon," the lady praises. "Worst part is over, okay? Just keep breathing. We're almost done."

She fills a few different vials with the blood, and Rory takes deep breaths in and out. I never let go of his hand.

"All done," she says, cheerfully, backing away. She returns with a cotton ball and some medical tape. "You can sit up when you're ready, but no rush."

He nods and stays still for a moment before he opens his eyes. "I think I'm good."

I stand and help him sit, so damn proud of my roomie I could squeeze the stuffing out of him. I don't, though. Just help him back into his jacket and let him hop off the table.

I do hug him to my side when we're walking away after thanking the nice phlebotomist. "You were great!" I tell him, then ruffle his hair as he smiles and squirms.

"Thank you for coming," he says, his cheeks flushed. "For making me feel safe."

"Of course, little dude." I hope I can always make him feel safe, that whatever happens he knows that with me, there's nothing but acceptance and love.

My sweet little rabbit.

RORY

Damn, I want to kiss this sweetheart of a hunky man so bad. He was so amazing. I've never felt more at ease with someone than I do with Parker.

After my appointment he offered to take me out for breakfast because I was fucking starving. I'm trying not to think of it as a date because I know it's really not, but god, I really wouldn't mind if it was.

Would he want someone like me, though? I mean, I know he finds me attractive, or at least he did until I lost it on him and left him with a hard on in a public bathroom. Maybe that attraction went out the window just like his orgasm. But even if he does find me desirable still, hooking up with me is one thing. Being friends with me is one thing. Being more, I don't know that he would want that. It's only been a month since I broke up with Zach and moved in with Parker, but I can honestly say it's been the best decision I ever made. The trouble is, I find myself wanting things with him that I'm not sure he wants, or will ever want. But I'm also realizing how much better my life is without Zach in it, and how much Parker's words and actions are invading my thoughts, to the point where Zach's aren't taking up the space they used to.

I pull out my phone as we sit at the booth in the local breakfast joint Parker took me to. There's not much on the menu that I can eat, but there are a few things. He's got a mouth full of eggs when he mumbles, "Whatcha doin?"

"Something I should have done a long time ago," I say, tapping at my screen before I set my phone down and look up at him. "Blocking Zach's number." I shake my hands out and let out a breath. God, I'm nervous, but I also feel incredibly liberated. I stopped reading any messages from him a long time ago, and honestly he hasn't sent me any in a while, but even though I know he's shit and I am better off without him, the idea of closing him out of my life for good was still scary. It's less scary now, though. Because I realize how much happier I am each and every day that he isn't in the picture.

"Hell, yeah, little dude," he cheers, raising his hand, and I smile widely as I give him a high five. I finish my oatmeal and coffee and when the waitress comes by with the check and hands it to Parker I flush.

"I can get mine," I tell him. He shakes his head.

"Not a chance. You were brave as hell today and you aren't paying for your own breakfast."

I bite my lip to keep from smiling, but don't argue with him as he pulls his wallet out. "Thank you," I tell him, and he grins at me.

I usually love my classes, but today, for whatever reason, okay, I know the reason, I'm eager to be finished and back home with Parker. I've missed him since we went our separate ways this morning.

It's late afternoon when I get back to our apartment, and Parker isn't there yet, so I decide to get some homework done and a little bit of cleaning. I vacuum, wash the dishes in the sink, and change the sheets on my bed. Then I decide that I've been sweating way too much and don't smell the best, and if I am going to be snuggling up against Parker tonight while we watch a movie, which I'm hoping will be the case, I need to shower.

I make my way into the bathroom and slide off my suspenders, then remove my bowtie before stripping off my shirt and pants. I'm half hard as I look at myself in the mirror and my cock twitches when I think of my sexy, adorable roommate. Those gorgeous muscles, that swoon worthy smile, and the way he takes care of me, looks after me. I moan as I reach down and stroke myself, picturing Parker on his knees for me again. Or letting me straddle him as I lick up his toned abs and suck on those insanely defined pecs and deliciously dark nipples.

"Oh, fuck," I whimper as precum leaks out and a wet spot forms on my underwear. God, I haven't jacked off in a while and it feels amazing. I take a quick break to strip out of my underwear and slide off my glasses, then turn the water to the shower on before I step inside and grip my dick again. It feels amazing, but I need more, so I reach over and pump some body wash on my hand, using it as lube as I stroke myself faster and harder, whimpering as I imagine Parker's big strong hand around me, his scent overwhelming me, his lips pressed to my wet skin as I thrust into his grip.

"Fuck!" I cry out. His name leaves my lips on a stifled moan as I bite my lip and shoot my release all over the shower wall. I'm breathing heavily as I brace myself against the tile for a second, my eyes closed, chest rising and falling.

Damn that was amazing, but it also makes me realize how much I want my roommate, and it scares me because the last time I got attached to someone it didn't go so well.

I know Parker is nothing like Zach. When Parker talks to me he looks at me, and listens. He supports me and encourages me. When he congratulates me on something, it's genuine. When he makes dinner for me he never complains about how inconvenient it is. He genuinely enjoys my friends instead of tolerating them at best, and has never said a single derogatory thing about either Lucy or Jackson, which Zach did on a regular basis, complaining about how clingy they were and how they took time away from us. Parker isn't my boyfriend but he still understands how important Lucy and Jackson are to me. He's never done anything to make me feel bad about myself or like I'm a burden in some way and he's just patient and tolerant enough to deal with me. Things that I believed for a really long time until Parker came along and showed me that my needs matter, too. That I'm worth the extra bit of effort.

I don't know what's scarier. Him not wanting me the way I want him, or something more happening between us, only for me to realize that he isn't who I thought he was, and being crushed all over again. I hate that Zach has taken away my ability to trust myself when it comes to relationships. And I hate that I didn't realize what he was doing and how he was manipulating me from the very beginning, but now I'm terrified of trusting anyone with my heart, feeling like I always have to have walls up, always have to be on the alert, in case the next person tries to take advantage of me, too.

I sigh and dry off, before slipping my glasses back on and grabbing my clothes. I pad down the hall to my bedroom and shut the door before tossing my dirty clothes in the hamper and sliding into sweats and a cropped T-shirt with a sleeping teddy bear wearing a nightcap on the front.

I hear dishes clanking together when I get closer to the living room/kitchen area and I can't help the grin that spreads across my face when I see Parker rummaging through the cupboards, wearing a bright green apron with sloths on it over his jeans and T-shirt. He pulls out a mixing bowl and I see the flour and sugar sitting next to him on the counter. There's also dairy free butter and some vegan chocolate chips.

"Hey, short stack," he says, beaming when he sees me. I flush when his gaze travels from my face down my body and back up, his own cheeks pinkening when his eyes meet mine again. "You, uh..." he clears his throat. "You look good. I like your shirt." He bites his lip and goes back to grabbing things from the different drawers and cupboards. Measuring cups and spoons, a spatula. I hear him mumble something that sounds like, "What was I looking for again?"

God, he's so cute, all flustered at the sight of me. And I can't help feeling a bit proud that he likes what he sees. I move to the bar and sit, watching him. "Everything okay?"

He looks back at me, briefly. "Yeah, of course. Why do you ask?"

"You said you bake when you're nervous or stressed."

"Oh, yeah, I do," he says as he starts filling the large bowl with the different ingredients. "I do it for fun, too, though, but I'm actually making these for a friend in one of my classes. She's having a hard time right now, some family stuff, and my chocolate chip cookies always cheer her up. I'm adjusting the recipe so you can have some, too." He flushes and grins at me.

Damn. Could he be any more perfect? "That's really sweet of you. I mean both doing it for her and me. Thank you."

He shrugs as he measures out some brown sugar and dumps the contents in the bowl. "It's no big deal. It's not much effort for something I know will make a difference. I can't do much else. I just wish she didn't have such a shitty family." He looks at me and winks. "And you deserve yummy treats, too."

My cheeks heat and I can't help grinning. "She's lucky she

has you," I tell him, and see the flush creeping up his neck and staining his cheeks pink as well.

"I'll make dinner when I'm done with these," he says.

"No rush," I tell him. "You wanna watch something tonight?" I'm really hoping he does, because I want to snuggle up against him more than anything, and it's the best excuse I've got to be that close. If I was more confident I'd just plonk myself right on his lap, but it takes all my courage just to rest my head on his shoulder. I was so nervous the other night, that he would tell me to move. But he didn't. I know he must have carried me to my bed, too, when I fell asleep against him, and part of me was pissed when I woke up and realized I'd missed it.

My heart gives a little pitter patter in my chest when he looks back at me and grins. "Sounds good to me."

The apartment smells like fresh baked chocolate chip cookies minutes later, and when they come out of the oven Parker sets a few aside, giving me a smile. I bite my lip. "If I'm good, can I have one after dinner?" I ask, and his eyes widen. My cheeks flame when I realize how that sounded. "Oh my god," I mumble, burying my face in my hands. "I'm gonna go die now." I start to slide off the barstool and Parker laughs as he sets the plate with three cookies down in front of me.

"You can have one now if you're really good," he says, and I smile, my face heating all over again when he winks at me.

I wait a few minutes for the cookie to cool down a tiny bit before I take a bite and moan at the gooey chocolatey goodness. "Oh, god, that's good." I lick my lower lip when I feel the warm, melted chocolate against it and my dick jumps in my sweats when I see the heat in Parker's gaze as he stares at me.

He clears his throat again as he turns away and wipes his hands – which are perfectly clean by the way – on his apron.

"I'll start dinner in a second," he tells me as he grabs the dirty utensils and starts piling them in the dishwasher.

"I'll do that," I tell him, jumping off my bar stool and moving around the counter into the kitchen. "You cook and I clean, remember?"

"That's just for dinner," he says, "not everything. And I made the mess."

I smile at him. "I don't mind. Let me help." I place my hand on his chest and shove him away, the feel of his firm body underneath my palm making me shiver. He nods and pulls out a baking dish before changing the temperature on the oven slightly. Then he grabs some chicken out of the refrigerator as I load the dirty dishes. I bite my lip when I see him sneaking glances at my ass out of the corner of my eye. And I might enjoy it a little too much.

"Shit," I hear and then a wince as something clatters, and turn to see Parker holding his finger, blood running down his hand.

"Fuck," I say and grab him, pulling him towards the sink. I turn it on and shove his finger under it. Then grab a washcloth and press it over the wound, and he winces again. "You okay?" I ask. He nods, but doesn't look at me. I tell him to hold the wash cloth over his finger while I get the first aid kit. His cheeks are flushed as I rinse the area around the wound with soap and water, being careful not to get the soap in the cut, before I pat his finger dry and then apply antiseptic ointment. Finally, I wrap a bandage around the injury, and before I can even think twice about it, I bring it to my lips and press a soft kiss to his finger.

Parker's breath hitches and my gaze meets his. God, I want to kiss him so badly. "Thank you," he murmurs, his eyes darting to my lips. His thumb rests against my bottom lip, his fingers under my chin, and I swallow as he draws closer to me. I'm pushing up on my tiptoes, getting ready to taste him again, finally, when my phone chimes loudly and Parker startles, releasing me. "I uh, I should get back to the chicken." He holds his finger up. "Thanks again."

I nod. Goddamn it. I'm going to murder whoever ruined that moment. When I finish loading the dishwasher I wash my hands and pick up my phone. I can't get too upset when I see Mom's sent me a picture of my little sisters playing dress up. There's a text underneath that says, **It's not the same without you**. I smile because I miss it, too. I used to play dress up with them all the time when I was at home, and they loved it. We'd break out their stuffed animals and have tea parties with real treats that we baked together.

Ava is wearing an Elsa dress and Addison is dressed up like Moana. They both have huge smiles on their faces as they look at the camera, their arms around each other.

Can't wait for Thanksgiving, I type back.

Parker puts dinner in the oven and tells me he's going to go take a shower. He still seems a bit flustered, and I hope things won't be too weird between us now. Fortunately, he seems a bit more himself when he returns to the kitchen, now in sweats and a tank. Fuck, that's so not fair. I feel my dick twitching again as I stare at those biceps, trying not to drool.

We eat dinner together on the sofa and Parker hands me the remote. "Wanna pick a documentary?" he says, and I grin. We watch *Sr*, which is a documentary on Robert Downey Sr. and Parker stands about twenty minutes in to take his plate to the kitchen. He comes back with a bag of potato chips and settles back into the sofa. I don't miss that he's quite a bit closer now than he was before, and that he's slouching.

I shuffle closer to him until my arm is pressed against his, my legs up on the sofa in the spot I was just sitting in.

I rest my head on his shoulder and breathe in his scent, my fingers aching to slide between his. I flinch when I hear him crunching on the potato chips a second later. I try to stay where I am but it's so loud with my ear right next to his jaw and I end up lifting my head.

As he chews, I feel my nerves fraying. I move a little bit

further away to try and help and he looks over at me. I give a small smile and he smiles back. "Want some?" he asks, holding the bag up. I shake my head and he shrugs, then shoves another fistfull of chips in his mouth.

I last another minute before I can't take it anymore. I know he's not actually chewing super loud but it sounds loud to me. He has his mouth closed and everything but it's still making me tense and irritable and I can't hear the show over the noise.

"Will you stop?" I almost shout all of a sudden, and he turns to look at me with wide eyes.

"Sorry," he says, except his mouth is full of chips and it comes out like "Thorry," as little bits of chip fly out all over his lap and the sofa.

I can't help laughing at how silly he looks, his mouth closed around the remainder of the chips as he tries not to chew anymore. "You can chew and swallow," I tell him. I can tell that he chews as little and as slowly as possible before I see his Adam's apple bob as he swallows. "I'm sorry. I know it's not fair. You should be able to eat without me getting so worked up. I'll leave so I don't bother you." I move to stand up but he rests his hand on my leg.

"Don't go," he says. "I'm done anyway."

I eye him. "You're not just saying that?"

He shrugs. "I mean, I could eat more, but I'd rather you be here with me."

I flush. "You shouldn't feel like you can't have a snack when I'm in the same room, though."

"We'll figure out something. I can have my snacks before or after we watch so I don't bother you. Or I can eat something softer."

I bite my lip and then climb off the couch to grab the handheld vacuum cleaner, as Parker starts dusting his pants off and then picking up the larger pieces from the floor and couch.

I bring it back to the living room and use it to clean up the remaining mess. I notice Parker sneaking off to his room with the bag of chips and when he comes back a few seconds later they're closed. He wasn't in there long enough to sneak any. God, I think he left so I wouldn't have to hear the crinkling of the bag when he closed it.

He moves towards the kitchen and returns the bag to the pantry as I place the vacuum back in the hall closet. Then we're heading to the sofa again and I don't hesitate to curl up next to him. He grins and slouches a little bit again, and I take the opportunity to rub my cheek against his shoulder. The next thing I know his warm, giant fingers are lacing with mine and I suck in a breath as my entire body tingles and my heart stutters in my ribcage.

"This okay?" he whispers, and I nod. He presses a kiss to my curls and he doesn't let go of my hand even for a second while we watch the rest of the show.

NINE

RORY

Two weeks have gone by since our almost kiss, and nothing more has happened. We cuddle almost every night on the sofa while we watch something, and Parker presses kisses to my hair and holds my hand each and every time. It's wonderful, but frustrating too, because we haven't talked once about what we're doing or what any of it means, and I'm starting to go crazy. But I can't bring myself to ask him either, because if he tells me it's nothing, I'll be devastated.

We're heading out soon for a Halloween party at one of the frat houses near campus, and I need to get my costume on.

I'm slipping into the black silk panties I decided to wear with my costume when I hear a knock on the door. I slide my robe on quickly before saying, "Come in."

The door opens and Parker is standing there with a basket full of laundry that I realize is mine. He walks in and sets it on the bed. "I hope it's okay I got your stuff out. I needed to start my stuff in the dryer before we left."

"Yeah, of course," I say, and then my face heats when his gaze catches on the drying rack at the foot of my bed with my costume draped over it, along with several pairs of lace and silk panties.

Without seeming to realize what he's doing, he steps closer and picks up the lacy orange pair. Fuck, I'm simultaneously aroused and terrified at the sight of Parker holding my panties.

I started wearing panties shortly after Zach and I got together. I wanted to find a way to spice things up in the bedroom, and discovered that they made me feel sexy and pretty, but when he made fun of me for them, I tucked them away and hadn't touched them since, until about a week ago when I decided I wanted to start wearing them again, for me. Because I liked them, the way they looked on me, the confidence I felt when I slipped them on, my cock and balls nestled against the silky, lacy material, and I didn't give a fuck what Zach thought, or at least I was trying not to. But if Parker responds to them the same way Zach did…I swallow.

He clears his throat. "Are, are these yours?" he asks, his voice deeper than normal as he turns to face me, and I almost gasp at the unmistakable heat in his gaze when his eyes meet mine. I nod. "Damn, freckles, that's hot." He stares at me for a moment and I have a feeling he's trying to picture the panties on me, which makes me flush and squirm.

I step closer and take the panties from his hands gently. "I'll just take these," I say, and his cheeks turn bright red.

"Oh, right, yeah, of course. Sorry. I'll uh, leave, I guess. You do, whatever you were doing."

"I'll be out in a few minutes," I tell him. He nods, seemingly at a loss for words, and scurries off.

I bite my lip and shut the door behind me, resting my head against it, letting out a breath.

Parker said my panties were hot. And the way he looked at me, at them, fuck. I couldn't help noticing the slight bulge in his jeans when he left, and I reach inside my robe to squeeze my own cock that's half hard. Shit, I don't have time to jerk off. I have to get ready. I groan and will my cock to settle, before grabbing my clothes for the party and slipping them on. The black mini skirt with fake fur around the bottom and a tail attached to the back goes first. Next is a cropped long sleeved black shirt that has the same fake fur around the wrists. I sit on my bed to slide the black thigh high tights on, then secure the orange collar around my neck before slipping the cat ear headband on. I look at myself in the floor length mirror attached to my bedroom wall and grin. Damn, I look good. I just need the cat make up and my shoes, and I'm good to go. I slide the black heels on and then traipse down the hall to the bathroom.

I apply eyeliner around my eyes and the dark circle to my nose. I'm in the process of applying the cat whiskers when I hear, "Holy fuck," and turn to see Parker standing there, open mouthed, staring at me. And holy fucking shit, I stare right back. I don't know when I've seen a sexier cowboy. He's got chaps on over his jeans, a leather vest, no shirt, so his gorgeous chest is on full display, and a bandana tied around his neck. The only thing he's missing is the hat.

"You look amazing," I say, making every effort possible not to reach out and touch his bare abdomen. Jesus, his abs have abs.

"Shit, freckles, I don't hold a candle to you," he says, and I see his fists clenching and unclenching at his sides. Is he trying not to touch me, too?

"You like it?" I say, stepping back from the sink and gesturing to my outfit. He swallows and nods.

"God, you're pretty." His voice is a low rumble that sends a shiver down my spine as he looks at me. My cock jerks in my panties and I have to hold back a squeak.

"You, too," I reply and then wince at my choice of words. Parker isn't pretty. He's fucking sex on legs. He doesn't seem to mind the compliment though, and grins at me.

"I'll be ready in a second," I say, holding up my eyeliner pencil, and he nods, moving away from the bathroom.

I emerge a few minutes later and see Parker now in his

cowboy hat and boots, waiting by the door. He's also got a jacket on over his vest and is holding mine in his hands.

He grins at me as I walk towards him in my heels, then opens the jacket and holds it out for me to slip into. Oh my god. Zach never did stuff like this for me. And Parker's still looking at me like he wants to devour me.

I pop my earplugs into my ears and he grins wider. "I'll probably only last an hour or so," I tell him. "But you don't have to come back with me."

He nods and offers me his arm. I'm blushing like crazy when we head out the door.

PARKER

Hot damn, my roomie is the sexiest fucking kitty cat I've ever seen. The skirt, and the fucking tights, and that crop top showing off his slender tummy. Fuck, I want to nibble on every inch of him. I've never seen him in a skirt before, but he looks scrumptious. And I still can't get over the sexy as fuck panties I saw in his room earlier. I can't believe I actually picked them up, but my brain went out the window as soon as I thought of Rory's cute little bottom in them, and I acted without thinking. Fortunately he didn't seem to mind too much.

This little dude keeps surprising me in the best ways, and I feel proud to be with him tonight as we walk through the front door of the frat house where the Halloween party is being held. There's two different stories with a winding staircase leading up to the second floor. The ground floor is packed with sweaty bodies and loud upbeat music resounds throughout the house as people talk, make out, and grind up against each other on the makeshift dance floor, aka, the living room. Guests have taken up seats on the furniture that has been pushed to the side to make room. It smells like alcohol, sweat, and weed.

I grip Rory's hand as we make our way through the crowd

and to the kitchen to get a drink. I don't plan on getting drunk, but I do want a little something.

We each grab a cider and move back through the throng of sweaty bodies, all wearing different costumes, as we make our way back to the living area. There's witches, nurses, angels, athletes, rock stars, a couple more cowboys, and a few animals, though no one comes close to looking as amazing as Rory.

I spot my friend Preston talking to Jackson and motion in their direction. Jackson is dressed in nothing but a bright green speedo and iridescent fairy wings, his pale skin on display. He's got glitter in his hair and around his eyes and he looks amazing. His tall, slender frame is perfect for the outfit. And it seems that Preston is quite taken with him, if the way he's looking at the other man is anything to go by.

"Do they know each other?" I ask Rory over the roar of the music.

"Not that I know of," Rory says, seeming just as surprised as me that they're talking. "I didn't know Preston was gay."

"He isn't," I say. "Not that I know, anyway." But hey, sometimes you don't even know yourself until you meet the right person. "Maybe it's not like that. Maybe they're just talking." We watch as Jackson laughs at something Preston whispered in his ear, and then Jackson is taking Preston's hand and pulling him through the crowd towards the stairs.

We exchange looks but don't get a chance to say anything before we hear, "Rory, fancy seeing you here. I thought you would be too ashamed to show your face in public from now on."

We turn and I know who I'm looking at without being told. Douchenozzle Zach and whatever flavor of the month he has on his arm.

Rory's eyes narrow. "Why would I be ashamed when I'm not the one who fucking cheated?"

Zach glares and steps closer. "Yeah, well, you'd cheat too if your partner was only putting out once a week and had a dick the size of a baby carrot. You're lucky I wasn't cheating sooner with what a lousy lay you were, you selfish little prick."

Rory's cheeks turn bright red and then he squeaks when Zach reaches out and grabs his crotch through his skirt. "Hey, back off," I snarl, shoving him back. "Keep your fucking hands to yourself."

Zach sneers at me. "This is cute," he says, glancing back at Rory and then me again. "You got yourself a guard dog."

"He's my roommate," Rory manages, but I can tell he's barely holding it together. "And he's right. Don't touch me."

Zach appraises him. "Wearing a fucking skirt, too? God, Rory, you're such a fucking pussy. Is that the only way you could get a guy? Trade your dick in for a cunt? You fucking him, too? Does he know what a fucking whore you sound like when you get plowed? How fucking embarrasing it is?"

Tears are filling Rory's eyes now and I've had enough. I take his hand and pull him with me down the hall as Zach laughs. I find the bathroom and sigh in relief when it's empty, pulling Rory inside and shutting the door behind me. I wet a washcloth and remove his glasses, setting them aside, before I dab at his tears. His eyeliner is running down his cheeks turning his tears black and my heart breaks for him. I want to go out there and squirt lemon juice in Zach's eyes for hurting Rory.

"Stop," he says, sniffling and batting my hand away. "You don't need to do that."

I frown. "But I want to. He didn't have any right to say those things."

"Maybe he does," Rory says. "Maybe he's right. After all, I've never been with anyone else. I can't even get a second opinion."

"He's an arrogant, stuck up, asshole who's trying to make you feel like shit about yourself, because if he can make you feel small and like you don't deserve better maybe you'll go crawling back to him, or maybe you'll just walk around miserable never trying to find someone better because you don't believe you deserve it. He's wrong, freckles. You're amazing and you deserve everything you want." I grip his chin and continue to dab at his tears. He blinks at me and his chest heaves slightly.

"You look incredible. You're the prettiest one out there. He's just jealous he doesn't have control of you any more." His eyes flick to my lips and I'm so tempted to close the space between us and kiss him like I've wanted to for weeks now, but I can't. Not when he's this upset. I haven't made a move so far because I don't want him to think I'm just using him for sex. He deserves better than that, and he's been through a lot. But god, it's been hard.

Instead I press a kiss to his curls and then turn his face towards the mirror. "Good as new," I say, and he gives me a soft smile.

"Thank you. I'm really, really embarrassed about all the shit he said. I'm so sorry, Parker."

I slip his glasses back on and shake my head. "No one in this room needs to be apologizing. Do you want to go?"

He shakes his head. "No. Then he wins. I can't let him ruin every public gathering for me. Let's get another drink."

We make our way out of the bathroom and fortunately don't spot Zach and his date anywhere as we move through the crowd back towards the kitchen. Rory grabs another cider but I stick to soda. I have a feeling I should keep an eye on him. He seems a little bit better, but I know Zach's words had an impact on him and I wouldn't be surprised if he drank more than normal tonight because of it.

I take out my phone and text Jackson and Lucy to make sure they know we're here and that Rory is upset. I don't give them details, just tell them that we ran into Zach.

I get a reply from Lucy right away. She says she's outside, and we make our way in that direction after grabbing our jackets. There's a fire pit set up in the backyard and even more people out here, drinking, talking, and some people are roasting marshmallows.

"Hey, Rory," Lucy says when we reach the firepit. I turn, startled. I almost don't recognize her since she's dressed up as Gamora from *Guardians of the Galaxy*, green skin and everything. She looks amazing, though, her normally curly hair straight and dyed red.

"Hey," he says. "You look great."

She smiles. "You, too." She looks at me. "And you look very yummy."

I flush. "Thanks."

We talk for a bit and I mention seeing Jackson and Preston together, which sparks her interest. Apparently none of us knows what's going on between those two.

"Time for another drink," Rory says about fifteen minutes later. He's shivering now, too, even with his jacket on.

That's the same moment another girl slides up next to Lucy, dressed as Merida from *Brave*, and starts flirting with her, so I take Rory inside and get him another drink.

"Last one," I tell him. "You're getting tipsy already." I had no idea he was such a lightweight, but I don't think he actually drinks that often, and he's tiny.

He takes it, his words already slurring slightly when he says, "I'm completely fine. I am better than fine. I am soooo fine."

I'm regretting letting him have the last bottle about ten minutes later when he's clearly not fine. "I think we should head home," I tell him as I take the drink from his hand and set it on the counter. I put my arm around his back and drape his arm over my shoulder, hunching as I try to support him. We take a few steps before he trips over something, probably his own feet. He wobbles on his heels and his knees buckle, but I manage to grab him before he falls, and he giggles.

"You are so strong," he says, his face turned towards me, the stench of alcohol on his breath. "So strong and so fucking hot." He pokes my bicep. "I mean, wow, just look at these muscles."

I move us through the crowd as he continues to jab me in the arm. "Okay," I say, once we reach the front porch. "Let's get you in the car." I'm honestly not sure he can make it down the stairs so I scoop him into my arms and carry him instead, prompting a gasp and then another giggle as he kicks his feet in the air.

"See," he says, "I told you you were strong. And hot. Soooo hot." He starts to stroke my bare chest and I shiver. "And sweet." His eyes meet mine and they fill with tears. "God, you're so damn sweet." He buries his face in my chest as he sobs. "You closed the chip bag in your room so I wouldn't hear it."

"Hey, it's okay, little dude," I try to soothe him. "You're gonna be okay." I set him down so I can open the car door and he wobbles again before his face pales and then he's turning his head and vomiting near the rear passenger side door. "Oh, boy. Okay. You feel better now?" I ask as he wipes his chin and then reaches for my belt.

"Miss your cock," he slurs as I ease him into the front seat and try to buckle him. "It was so big and beautiful, not like my teeny weeny one." He puts emphasis on the words and holds his thumb and forefinger up about an inch apart. Then his head lolls to the side. "You know Zach was right about that. I have a baby carrot cock. I can't believe you ever wanted me." He sniffles again and more tears slide down his cheeks. "You did, you know? That first night? You gave me that blow job, and I don't know why because my cock is so tiny it's not much good for anything. And then I ran away, and you haven't wanted me since then. I don't blame you. I'm not very good in bed."

I honestly don't have a clue what to say to all of his jibber jabber, but I'll admit some of it makes me sad. I hate to hear him talk about himself like that, even if he is drunk. That Zach buttface really did a number on him and his self esteem, and he's so sweet, and cute, and smart, and talented, it just boils my biscuits that anyone could be so mean to him or make him feel badly about himself. I get him buckled and close the door before making my way around to the driver's seat.

It's a short drive and we're home in less than ten minutes. I park the car and hurry around to help him out. "Carry me," he says and throws his arms around my neck.

"Sure, little dude." I scoop him in my arms again and he kicks his feet and lets out a "weee!!!"

"Can you open the door?" I ask him when we get to the main entrance. He reaches out and pulls on it, then cheers again as I make my way up the stairs with him in my arms. He's tiny, but hauling him up three flights of stairs while he seems to be doing his best to catapult himself out of my arms is not easy.

I get us inside, and as soon as I set him on his feet he's running down the hall. I hear him vomiting again seconds later. Oh boy. This could be a long night, and I don't want to leave him alone.

I find him kneeling on the bathroom floor with his cheek resting against the toilet seat and I cringe. He managed to get most everything in the toilet, unfortunately that includes his kitty cat ears. Fuck, I'm the best roommate ever. I wipe off his chin and then pick him up again and carry him to my bed. It's bigger than his, and like I said, I don't want to leave him alone. I grab some rubber gloves and slide them on before fishing the kitty ears out of the toilet and flushing everything else down. Then I try to clean and disinfect the ears as best I can before leaving them on a towel in the kitchen to dry.

After that I grab a glass of water and take it to the bedroom along with a breath mint. His eyes are lidded and he groans as I push him up on the bed. "You need to drink," I tell him, and hold the glass to his mouth. He manages to get a few sips in and then lets out a huge burp.

"Oh, jeez, that was bad," he says, waving his hand in front of his face. "Sorry."

"Don't worry about it," I tell him. "Here, suck on this." He takes the breath mint and pops it in his mouth.

"Woah, that's good," he says, his eyes widening, like I just gave him weed or something.

"Keep sucking," I say. "Don't swallow it whole." I don't mind letting him share my bed, but if he's going to be this close to me I'd like to try and avoid the smell of vomit and cider. I hope that doesn't make me a terrible person.

He gives me a grin and a thumbs up sign as he sucks and I move down the bed to slip his shoes and tights off. He starts to giggle again and I look at him. "What is it?"

He giggles more. "You're undressing me."

I chuckle. "Yeah, I guess I am, but don't get excited. I'm stopping there." I move up to the head of the bed and slide his glasses off, setting them on the nightstand next to him, then help him lie down again.

He reaches out and grips my arm. "Don't wanna be alone," he murmurs, those big blue eyes gazing up at me.

"I'm not gonna leave you, short stack," I promise. "I do need to get you one of your nose things, though. Where are they?"

"Nightstand," he murmurs, and I leave the room, returning with the nasal strip and handing it to him. He fumbles with it for a bit before pouting and handing it back to me. I chuckle a little, then tear it open. It's really similar to a bandaid wrapper, and I pull off the backing, before reaching over and placing it across his nose.

"Good?" I ask, and he nods.

I start to undress myself and he stares at me. I really don't mind, so I don't bother leaving the room. I strip out of my costume until I'm down to my boxer briefs and then slide into pajama pants before climbing into bed next to him. He immediately rolls over to face me and scoots closer.

"You take such good care of me," he says, resting his head on my chest and stroking his fingers over my abdomen.

"Boop," he says, when he gets to my belly button and pokes it. Jesus, he's a strange drunk.

He lifts his head and stares at me. "I want you to kiss me," he says. "I want you to fucking kiss me. And I want you to fuck me." He frowns and keeps tracing my abdomen with his finger. "You probably don't want that, though. I'm lousy in bed. That's what Zach says. You heard him, didn't you? You were there when he said what a lousy lay I am. How I moan like a whore. He said it was embarrassing." His eyebrows furrow. "He did nothing but insult me and then wondered why I wanted sex less and less. And I spent so long trying to be better for him. Trying to be what he wanted me to be. And he still cheated."

He rests his head on my chest and I hear his sniffles as his body shakes slightly against me. "'It's a good thing you have a hole because your dick isn't good for much, is it?' That's what he said. I was lucky he wanted me for as long as he did. No one wants me."

I have tears filling my eyes as I squeeze him against me. That jerk face said all those horrible things to my sweet Rory and he has spent the last two months trying to believe something different. To believe he's worthy and desirable. He has no idea how desirable he is, because Zach fucking shattered his self esteem, just to make himself feel better, to keep Rory under control, to make him feel like no one else would want him. But it's just not true.

I fucking want him.

"Shh," I soothe, stroking my fingers through his hair. "Sleep, little dude."

He's snoring softly a moment later.

TEN

RORY

I groan when the sun shines on my eyes, drawing me out of sleep the following morning. I have a headache but it's not as bad as it could be. Flashes of the night before start to play through my head and I realize I don't remember most of what happened after we got to the Halloween party. I remember Zach, but after that it's all a bit of a blur.

I open my eyes and start when I realize I'm not in my own bed. I jolt up and look around before I see Parker next to me, and I don't know if I should feel relieved or horrified. What the hell happened last night? Then my eyes widen when I look down and see what I'm wearing. It's a T-shirt, but it's not mine. It's huge on me.

Fuck. Parker wouldn't take advantage of me, I know that, but why am I in his clothes? I still have my black panties on underneath, and god his shirt smells amazing, and it's ridiculously soft.

"Hey," I hear and turn to see Parker blinking up at me. "How are you feeling?"

"Um, okay, I think," I say. I pull on the shirt. "Is this yours?"

He flushes. "Yeah. You threw up in the middle of the night and a little bit of it got on your costume. I figured you wouldn't want to sleep in it after that. This was the easiest thing to get you into. I hope that's okay?"

I groan and fall back on the pillow, my hands over my eyes. "Okay, yes, but mortifying."

He chuckles. "We've all been there. It's no big deal. I rinsed off your costume and put it in the wash but didn't start it. I didn't know how to wash it."

"God, what else did you do?" I ask, turning towards him. "I don't remember much."

He flushes again. "It doesn't matter. You would have done the same for me." He pauses, then says, "We didn't do anything last night, just so you know. I mean, nothing happened. You just slept in here."

I flush, then nod as I bite my lip. "I didn't say anything too awkward or embarrassing, did I?"

"Um, no," he says, but I can tell by the hesitation in his voice and the way his eyes flit away from mine he's full of it.

"Oh, god," I groan, covering my face with my hands again. "You're a terrible liar. What did I say?"

He chuckles. "I mean, it wasn't that bad. Just that you thought I was hot…" he trails off.

I peek out from behind my hands. "That's not so bad."

He bites his lip. "And that you wanted me to kiss you."

My cheeks flame. "Oh, god." I hide again. "What else? Just get it over with so I can go walk into traffic."

He laughs. "You might have mentioned something about wanting me to fuck you. And a few more things that I don't think are worth repeating."

I move my hands away from my face and stare at him. "Why aren't they worth repeating?"

I shiver when he reaches over and strokes my cheek. "Because they aren't true."

I swallow. "You don't know that."

He gives a small smile. "I'm pretty certain. I only had a

few minutes with you that night at the club, short stack, but it was enough to make me want more."

Tears fill my eyes and I hurry to wipe them away, sniffling as I do. "He said –" I'm cut off by Parker's finger against my lips. He shakes his head.

"Don't repeat it. Don't listen to it. Don't believe it. He was a manipulative narcissist who thought he could use you, and make you feel so bad about yourself that even after he cheated on you you would go back to him. And when that didn't work he got pissed, and now he's just out to hurt you more. That doesn't say anything about you, but it says a lot about him."

I nod, and then Parker's hand is sliding to my cheek, and his eyes are flitting to my lips. He moves closer and my heart starts pounding, goose bumps breaking out across my skin.

Right before he kisses me, though I put my finger to his lips. "I can't," I say. He frowns. "I need to brush my teeth. I feel gross."

I grab my glasses off the nightstand and slip them on before I slide out of bed and make my way down the hall towards the bathroom. I wasn't lying when I said I wanted to brush my teeth. I'm sure my breath is disgusting after last night. But I'm also trying to screw up the courage to let him kiss me. Yes, I've wanted it for a long time, but after last night I'm more anxious than ever about Parker rejecting me. I'm also scared of it leading to something more, because even though I don't want to let Zach's words bother me, they do, and what if Parker realizes that he was right? That I'm a lousy lay? What if he doesn't like the noises I make when I'm being pleasured? What if I humiliate myself?

I only had a few minutes with you that night at the club, short stack, but it was enough to make me want more.

I brush my teeth and remove my nasal strip, tossing it in the trash, then head to the kitchen for a glass of water. I'm swallowing it down when Parker comes around the corner looking as sexy as ever in his pajama pants and no shirt, his dark hair tousled, and his dick tenting his pants.

I almost whimper as he steps closer to me, because I want him so fucking badly, but I'm still scared. He takes the glass from my hand, setting it on the counter behind me. "I brushed my teeth, too," he says. "But if you don't want this, just tell me."

You look incredible. You're the prettiest one out there. He's just jealous he doesn't have control of you any more.

I shake my head as he steps closer. His brows furrow. "Is that a no, or –"

"No," I say, softly, urgently. "I mean, no. I mean, it's not a no."

He grins. "Yes?"

I nod. The words are a whisper when I say them. "Yes. Yes. Kiss me. Please fucking kiss me."

He grips both of my cheeks in his giant hands and slots his lips against mine. He's gentle, and slow and so unbelievably sweet and tender. I slide my arms around his neck, and his arms move down, wrapping around my waist as I push up on my tiptoes to reach him better. I kiss him back, gasping when he grips my thighs and hauls me up, setting me on top of the counter. Our lips part for a moment and I stare at him, his hazel eyes dark, pupils blown wide, his cock fully tenting his pajama pants now. There's even a wet spot where his precum has leaked through. Oh, fuck. It's hard for me to believe that it's me that's doing that to him.

"You okay?" he asks, his voice gruff, and I nod. His mouth meets mine again. He kisses harder now, his tongue sliding along my lower lip, and I hesitate before letting him inside. I'm whimpering in an instant as he devours me, sucking and licking on my tongue, running his fingers through my hair. I moan when he presses a hand against my back and slides me forward so that I'm pressed against him, my cock hard against his stomach. Oh, fuck that feels good. I start to rut against him and he moans, making my cock jerk.

Oh, fuck. Oh, fuck. I pull back and bury my face in his shoulder as I bite my lip, trying to stifle my whimpers and trembling. But I can't stop moving. It feels too damn good. I cling to him as I thrust.

"Hey," he says, stepping back and tilting my chin up to look at him. I almost sob at the lack of friction against my cock and have to keep myself from humping the air. "Don't hold back, freckles. I want it all. I want you to make yourself feel good, okay? I want you to nut so hard you pass out, and I don't want you to hide anything from me. I want all your pretty little noises. You feel good, I want to hear it. Okay?"

I nod and then grab his hips, pulling him back to me and wrapping my legs around his waist this time, letting the T-shirt I'm wearing slide up my thighs. "Don't move," I tell him, then grip his face and kiss him hard as I thrust my hips shamelessly against him. I moan into his mouth when I feel his warm, strong hands gripping my bare legs and then sliding under the shirt and pressing against my back.

"Nnnggg," I whine, clinging to him as I use his firm, muscled body to get myself off. "Oh fuck, Parker. Fuck. I'm so hard." I kiss him again, hard, and he returns the kiss, sucking and nibbling, tasting me. We moan into each other's mouths, our fingers running through each other's hair. I whimper when he tugs on my curls and my cock jerks. I pull back from the kiss, my hips still moving and my cock leaking like crazy in my panties. "I'm gonna come."

"Fuck, yes," he growls. "Come for me, little rabbit. You're so fucking hot when you're turned on. Don't stop."

God, he's amazing, and his encouragement only spurs me on. Our lips meet again and I shiver when he runs his finger up and down my spine, stopping just above the waistband of my panties each time. I thrust harder, moaning louder as his tongue tangles with mine again. "Oh, fuck," I moan. "Oh fuck, oh fuck, oh fuck. I'm gonna… fuck, Parker." I cling to him as my orgasm crashes into me and I'm spraying my release, filling up my silky black panties with my cum. I feel it sliding down my thighs seconds later.

"Damn, freckles, that was hot," Parker murmurs as I grip his shoulders and rest my head against him, breathing heavily. Then he sinks to his knees and raises my shirt just a bit more, before his fingers slide under the waistband of my panties. "Can I?"

My eyes widen but I lean back and let him slide them off, my naked ass now perched on the counter. He drops the cum covered panties on the floor. Then he leans forward and I suck in a breath, gripping his dark hair as he licks up my spunk, my thighs trembling, and I feel tears springing to my eyes.

His gaze meets mine after he's cleaned up every last drop. "You have the prettiest, most perfect cock in the world," he tells me, then presses a kiss to the tip, making it twitch. "I've thought that since the very first night."

"It's small," I tell him, my throat tight.

"It is," he says. "But so are you, little dude. And it's perfect for you. Don't let anyone tell you differently. Not even yourself. It's adorable, and I'm as crazy about it as I am about you." He kisses it again and again, then nuzzles it, and I have tears sliding down my cheeks when I pull him to his feet and kiss him again. I can taste myself on him and it's incredible.

"Let me blow you," I tell him, knowing he's still rock hard. This is the first sexual encounter I've had where the focus was solely on me, on my pleasure, on making sure I felt good. And it was incredible. I want to do the same for him.

"You don't have, to, freckles," he says, stroking my cheek. I smile.

"I want to, though." I hop off the counter and blush when I see my cum soaked panties lying next to his feet. Then I'm sinking to my knees on the hard floor as I pull his pajama pants and briefs down, letting them pool at his feet, his huge cock standing at attention between his legs and leaking profusely. I lick my lips as my dick jumps, trying to spring back to life. I stare up at him, realizing this is the first time he's been completely naked in front of me. Damn. I can't get enough of his gorgeous, toned body and all that golden skin, his thick thighs dusted with dark hair and the light treasure trail leading to his beautiful cock. My dick twitches again and I lean in, nuzzling his groin. His breath hitches as he grips my curls.

"Fuck, why is it so hot to have you on your knees for me, wearing my clothes, with your panties on the floor next to you coated in your cum?" he says, his voice husky. I smirk up at him, then lick the tip of his cock, the taste of him exploding on my tongue. I moan and close my eyes, then lick the tip again.

"I won't run away this time," I promise. "I want to swallow you. Come in my mouth."

"Are you sure?" he asks, ever the sweetheart. I nod, then hear him grunt as his grip on my hair tightens when I lick a stripe up his shaft, one hand gripping his hip and the other gripping his dick. I reach between his legs and fondle his balls, and he moans, spurring me on. I press my lips to his sack and kiss him before taking them in my mouth. "Oh, fuck, freckles, that's good."

I hum around him and suck for a bit longer before popping off. His dick is leaking like a sieve now, and I can't help feeling proud of myself for that. I grip it again and lick from base to tip before taking him into my mouth. He grunts and his hand leaves my hair. I look up to see him gripping the counter behind him, his face flushed and his pupils blown wide.

"Fucking fudgsicles, little man, you're sexy as hell," he rumbles, staring down at me. I take him deeper and watch as he throws his head back and his stomach sinks in, his knuckles turning white as he grips the counter harder. I moan at the taste of him, the weight of his thick, heavy cock on my tongue, filling me, the saltiness of his precum leaking out and sending zings of pleasure down my spine when it hits my tastebuds. I bob up and down, stroking him with my free hand and hearing his breath stuttering as he tries to keep from thrusting into me. His hand grips my hair again as he pants, and he pulls me off.

"I'm close," he tells me. "Can I move? Can I fuck your mouth, little rabbit?"

I nod. It's been a long time since I had someone face fucking me, but I've always loved both giving and receiving blow jobs and I want to make this good for him. I want to make him fall apart with my mouth. I take him deeper still.

"Oh, fuck. Yes, yes, fuck, freckles, I'm close. So fucking close." He thrusts into me, gripping my curls and making my eyes water as his dick slides in and out relentlessly. He stares at me and I know I must look like a sight, tears sliding down my cheeks, snot on my face as I breathe through my nose and let him use me. "Fuck, freckles, you look so good," he says. "I'm gonna come." He thrusts two more times and then he's throwing his head back as his body spasms, his thighs trembling as he shoots down my throat. I gag as I try to swallow everything, and some of his spunk slides out of my mouth and down my chin.

He pulls out and immediately slides to the floor, taking my face in his hands. "Shit, are you okay? That was intense. Did I hurt you?"

I shake my head as he uses the dish rag in his hands to wipe the mess from my face. "You were amazing," he tells me and I can't help beaming.

"You wanna shower with me?" he asks. "Or by yourself. No pressure, of course."

I smile. "I'd like that." He helps me stand and we make our way to his room and the master bath. I stare at him as he turns the water on, that tight ass on display, the corded muscles of his back flexing with every movement.

"Damn," I say, and he turns, grinning at me. I flush and bite my lip.

"Can I?" he asks, stepping closer and gripping my glasses.

I nod, and he slides them off, setting them on the counter, before he grips the shirt I'm wearing, and meets my eyes. I nod again, and my flush deepens as I raise my arms. He slides the shirt up and off, letting it fall to the floor. I feel a bit self conscious standing in front of him naked. I know I'm scrawny. I don't have muscles like he does and I definitely don't have a six pack. But the way he's looking at me tells me I don't need any of that to be sexy in his eyes.

"Damn, little rabbit," he says, his gaze heated once again. "I can't get over how fucking pretty you are." He bends to kiss me again and then tugs me into the shower.

We take our time rinsing off before Parker squirts some soap on his hand and starts to lather up my arms and shoulders. "This okay?" he asks. I nod. He moves his hands down my chest, bending over to reach my hips and belly. His hands are gentle, and I shiver as his breath ghosts over my naked skin. A gasp leaves me when his fingers caress my cock. He's not trying to turn me on, but it feels good nonetheless. He cleans me, and it feels almost worshipful, the attention he lavishes on my dick and my balls. After all the comments Zach made about my small penis, I stopped even undressing with him in the room because I became so self-conscious about it, but once again Parker is turning the tables, showing me how much he adores those parts of me that Zach sneered at.

"Oh, fuck," I whisper when he sinks to his knees and soaps up my legs, and then my feet. He presses a kiss to my belly button and then my cock, and fuck, I'm going to cry again if he doesn't stop being so damn perfect.

"Turn around," he instructs, and I do. He gathers more soap on his hands and washes my back. I can't help the moan that leaves my lips when his hands reach my ass cheeks, kneading them, before I feel his lips against my ass and the scruff of his stubble, making me suck in a breath. He stands and presses a kiss to my neck. I shiver when he rumbles in my ear, "You've got the cutest little ass, freckles."

I soap up my own hands next and wash him off. It takes longer because he's so damn big, but I manage. Then we rinse off and step out. He hands me a towel, and when I'm dry I wrap it around my waist. "I'll be right back," I tell him. "I'm gonna go change."

He nods and I slide my glasses back on before I head down the hall to my room. Holy shit. That just happened. All of it. I've been wanting it to happen for months and it did. We made out like teenagers and I came in my panties from rubbing off on him, and then I blew him, and holy fuck. Every single second of it was amazing.

I can't stop smiling when I make it to my room and drop the towel. I'm about to slip into a pair of briefs when I remember Parker's reaction to my panties yesterday, and the pair that's still on the floor in the kitchen covered in my cum. I slip into a pair of sparkly turquoise panties that have a small bow in the front and are sheer in the back, making my ass look amazing. *You've got the cutest little ass, freckles.*

I pull on a pair of gray sweats and then a cropped T-shirt with a rainbow across the front, before picking up my towel and making my way back to his room. He's dressed in sweats, too, and no shirt, water droplets falling from his hair and sliding down his torso, over his nipple, and along his abs, disappearing under the band of his sweats. Jesus.

"Damn," he says when he sees me. I may have dressed like this on purpose after noticing the way he looked at me the last couple of times I wore crop tops, and I can't help the smile that breaks out across my face as he stares at me. "I love the bow ties and suspenders, little dude, but you look scrumptious like this, too."

"Thank you," I say. I pout slightly when he slips a shirt on, but don't say anything. Asking him to walk around shirtless so that I can ogle him might be a little weird. And I probably wouldn't get much homework done.

"Breakfast?" he says. I nod and we make our way to the kitchen. I flush when I see my panties still on the floor and bend over to pick them up, grinning at Parker because I can't help myself. He grins back and his cheeks turn a rosy pink. I toss them in the wash along with my Halloween costume and set the washing machine to the delicate cycle.

After eating waffles and bacon, and finishing off two cups of coffee, I'm feeling a bit more like myself, and also very full, but I really don't have too bad of a hangover. Just a mild headache.

We decide to make a grocery run, and when we get back and everything is unloaded, we take out our homework. We work separately for a while, me at the bar on my laptop and Parker on the couch with his, before we switch to reading and I shuffle over to him.

"Can I?" I ask, shyly, and he beams, patting his lap.

I settle on the couch with my head in his lap and he grins down at me, stroking his fingers through my hair. He continues his gentle ministrations as we both read. I hum when he starts to scratch my scalp lightly. I remember when he gave me that scalp massage the night I felt so overwhelmed and overstimulated by the noise, and I sigh, closing my eyes and lowering my book.

He chuckles. "You like this, huh?"

I nod, opening my eyes. "It feels really good. Relaxing."

He grins, then leans down and presses a kiss to my lips. It's way too short, but then he's back to massaging my scalp and I close my eyes again.

"Hey, freckles," I hear a moment later, and blink my eyes open as I feel fingers against my scalp again. "I gotta make dinner."

"Hmm?" I say, blinking up at Parker. He grins at me.

"You fell asleep, little dude."

"Oh, sorry," I say, rubbing my eyes.

"No worries. You seemed like you needed it so I let you rest, but it's six o'clock and I'm starving, and I gotta pee."

I flush and grin, before sitting up and stretching. Parker's gaze lands on my abdomen as my crop top rises, and my grin widens when his eyes darken. He clears his throat, then scoots off the couch and heads into his room.

He let me sleep for an hour on his lap. And I managed a nap even without having one of my nasal strips on, which rarely works. I must have been tired.

Parker makes a broccoli and chicken casserole for dinner while I get back to my reading. Then we sit on the couch to eat while we watch *The Big Bang Theory*.

I snuggle up against him when I'm finished and he slides his hand in mine again, beaming at me and pressing a kiss to my hair. God, I'm horny, and being around him, breathing in his scent and feeling his palm against mine, sliding my finger up and down his arm and feeling those muscles under my finger tips, is just making me want him all over again. I don't think I've stopped wanting him all day, but it feels more like a need now than anything else. My cock is hard and aching in an instant and I'm whimpering as I nuzzle his shoulder and try to keep from humping the air.

"Kiss me," I say.

He turns to me. "Huh?"

"Kiss me," I repeat, more urgently. "God, I'm horny as fuck. Please, kiss me."

His eyes widen but he doesn't hesitate. He grips my cheek and slots his lips against mine. I'm moaning and whimpering instantly as his tongue delves inside my mouth. Turning, I push myself up on my knees to get a better angle. His arms wrap around me as I press into him, kissing him fiercely, my cock throbbing and precum leaking out onto my panties.

"Damn, little rabbit," he says, his voice hoarse when he pulls away for some air. His eyes are wide and his lips swollen, his chest rising and falling as he stares at me.

"Too much?" I ask, my anxiety spiking as I shrink back. He grips me and pulls me back towards him.

"Hell no," he rumbles, then kisses me again, taking me with him as he falls onto his back. We both moan as I straddle him and our hard cocks rub against each other through our pants.

Our kissing intensifies, and my jaw is sore from doing so much of it, but I can't stop. It's so good, and the feel of his cock brushing against mine over and over as we rub against each other is so fucking amazing. I can't stop whimpering and whining, rutting against him even harder when his hands grip my waist and he thrusts up into me. A zing of pleasure shoots down my spine and I gasp, pulling away.

"Come here," he almost growls, and pulls me up his torso so that I'm straddling his chest now.

"Oh, fuck," I breathe, when he lifts his head and begins to lick and suck along my belly. I use one hand to grip the back of the couch as I watch him, feeling that warm, wet tongue on my bare skin and how eager he is to devour me. "Nnngg," I whine, as my cock jerks in my pants. "Fuck, Parker."

"Can I mark you?" he asks, and holy hell my cock jerks. He wants to mark me?

"Yes," I say, and shove my bare stomach closer. He growls and rests his head back as I support myself on the arm of the sofa and bend over him. I rub my dick against his chest as he sucks and licks, then bites along my belly. I shake when I feel his tongue delve into my belly button. "Oh, oh, oh," I whimper. "I'm gonna come, Parker, fuck."

I rut against him again and again. He sucks harder. I throw my head back as pleasure consumes me, and I spray my release, coating my panties in cum for the second time that day.

"Fuck, yes, freckles," Parker says. "That was so fucking hot." He kisses me again, then says, "Take your pants and undies off for me? Don't let the cum slide out."

I blink, but shuffle down his legs and slide them off. I don't know what he has planned, but damn I want to find out. He lifts his hips and slides his pants and underwear down, then reaches out and says, "panties," his voice rough and eager. I hand them to him and watch with wide eyes as he takes the panties and slicks his cock up with my cum, before gripping his dick with the panties and stroking himself hard and fast.

Holy shit, that's hot. He's coated in my release and jerking himself off with my panties. I can't stop staring, and my dick is springing back to life as I watch.

"Oh, fuck," he grunts, and I can tell he's close. He leans forward and asks, "can I come on you?" I nod and lay back and he bends over me, still gripping my panties as he strokes himself faster and harder.

I grip my own dick and stroke myself. Seconds later he's letting out a guttural groan and spraying all over my abdomen and pelvis, and some even gets on my shirt, but it's all I need to come a second time, crying out his name as I do.

"Fuck," he breathes, staring down at me, and our cum mixed together on my torso. "That was insanely hot, little rabbit."

I nod. "Yeah," is all I manage. He bends over and kisses me, then stands and pulls his pants up before moving into the kitchen and coming back with a wet washcloth. He stops when he reaches me and stares at my upper body.

"Damn, you look really good like that, short stack. Stretched out on the couch in just your cute little top and covered in our cum."

I bite my lip and run my fingers through my hair, before swiping a finger through the mess on me and licking it off. "We taste good together," I say, and his eyes flare. I swipe more of our jizz off my belly and motion for him to come closer. He does and kneels next to me, opening his mouth. I put my finger inside and he closes around me, moaning as he sucks and licks. Then he's moving closer still and lapping up even more of the cum from my body, swallowing it down. He feeds me some more and I lick it off his finger this time. Then he's using the washcloth to get the rest of it off.

"I think you might need another shower," he says, blushing as he stands. I grin.

"You want to find a pair of panties for me to wear when I'm done?" I ask, arms above my head, body stretched out for his viewing. His eyes flare again.

"Really?"

I nod. "And maybe a T-shirt of yours? If that's okay?"

"Hell, yeah," he says, adjusting himself in his pants.

I climb off the couch and slip my crop top over my head. I can't remember ever having this much confidence, in any area of my life, but Parker makes me feel safe and desired and adored in a way that has it bursting out of me. I press up on my tiptoes to kiss him, before I saunter naked to the bathroom.

When I get out of the shower I see a pair of lacy yellow panties folded neatly on the counter with one of Parker's T-shirts underneath. I grin and dry myself off before slipping into them. The panties are lace in the back and don't quite cover my ass cheeks all the way, and satin in the front. They're incredibly soft and I feel sexy as hell wearing them. I bite my lip when I look in the mirror and see the marks he left. There's half a dozen of them scattered along my belly and torso, and I fucking love it. Might have to stay away from crop tops in public for a while, though. And I know if Jackson or Lucy saw them I would never hear the end of it.

I slip into Parker's shirt, which smells like him. It makes me want to lift it to my nose and breathe it in, so I do. It's huge on me, hitting me a couple of inches above the knees, the sleeves reaching my elbows. It's nothing special, just plain black, but I love it.

I make my way out of the bathroom and find Parker sitting on the couch, reading. He looks up at me and his cheeks pinken. I grin and bite my lip.

"You look good," he tells me. "Wanna watch something?"

Yes. But what I really want to do is show off my panties. Does he not want to see them? Or is he just too much of a gentleman to ask? Is offering to show my roommate my panties slutty, or inappropriate? I don't know, but I find myself not caring. I've dealt with too much shame over sex, feeling like I wasn't good enough, like my body wasn't good enough, like I didn't deserve to feel good or feel sexy because that's how Zach made me feel whenever we were together, especially the last few months, and I'm done with it. So even though I'm a little nervous, I say, "Can I…can I show you my panties first?"

My skin prickles with nerves, but they disappear when he stares at me and says, "You want to?"

I nod.

"Fuck, yeah," he says in that low rumble that has a shiver running down my spine and my cock twitching. God he has to stop using that voice, stop looking at me the way he is, or I'll run out of panties really fast. "I don't think I'll ever not want to see you in your panties, little rabbit."

I grin and flush as I reach down and raise the shirt he gave me, swaying my hips slightly and moving closer to him as I showcase my panties.

"Holy guacamole," he breathes, and I see his dick thickening in his sweats. "You're so fucking pretty, short stack."

I turn so he can see the way the lace lays against my cheeks, and I hear an audible groan. Then his hands are gripping my waist and he's hauling me back. I gasp, laughing as I land on his lap, my legs spread so I'm straddling him backwards, then moan when his lips press against my neck and he breathes me in. My dick jumps to life and I reach my arm back, wrapping it around his neck as he sucks and nibbles on my neck and shoulder.

"Fucking fruitcake, I can't get enough of you," he murmurs. His hands skate under my shirt and rest against my belly, holding me to him as I moan, one hand moving up my body and rubbing my nipple, making me buck and shout. He purrs against my neck, then licks the skin there before nibbling again, while at the same time pinching my nipple ever so slightly between his thumb and forefinger, rolling it.

"Oh, oh, fuck," I cry. "Parker, fuck." I had no intention of going another round but god, this feels good, and I can't stop. I've never been touched like this before. And those sounds he told me he wanted to hear, they are leaving my mouth unbidden now. "Oh, god, oh, fuck, nnnggg." I thrust my hips forward, searching for friction and the hand that was resting against my belly moves down, sliding inside my panties and gripping me. I let out something between a wail and a moan as he plays with my dick and balls, his other hand now rubbing circles on my nipple, making my cock jerk, his mouth an incessant force on my neck and shoulder as he sucks and licks.

"That's it, little rabbit," he murmurs. "Make all the pretty noises for me."

My entire body shudders at his words, my cock throbbing. I feel his hard dick against my ass and rut back against it, then thrust forward into his hand. He groans as I repeat the motion over and over. "More," I whine. "God, Parker, please, I need more." I'm fucking close to tears with how incredible this feels and I want to come so badly but I don't want it to be over.

He strokes me faster and harder, thrusting into me and pinching my nipple as he bites down on my neck, and my orgasm rolls through me in waves, my spunk shooting out all over his hand and drenching my panties once again.

I hear him let out a groan and feel his body tensing underneath me, then a pool of warmth against my backside before he relaxes. He chuckles against my neck. "Sorry. Maybe you should wear less sexy panties, or not show me the next pair."

I grin, still trying to catch my breath. "Don't ever apologize for making me come that hard," I tell him, and he laughs, kissing my hair. His hand slides out of my panties and I stand. Then we both head into our rooms to change. I slide into another pair of panties. These are bright pink, and I tell myself I won't show Parker. I've come three times today already, and I don't think I have a fourth orgasm in me anyway. The shirt Parker lent me is damp with sweat, but no cum got on it, so I leave it and head back out to the living room.

Parker has changed, too, and I curl up against him on the sofa as he turns on Netflix.

When our movie is over he kisses the side of my head and says, "You're welcome to sleep in my bed again tonight, or any night for that matter. But no pressure. I want you to feel comfortable."

"I'd like to sleep in your bed," I tell him, and he beams at me. "Just let me brush my teeth first? And put on a nasal strip. And grab my sleep mask."

When I get to his room a few minutes later he's in bed already, his shirt off, and I climb in next to him, scooting over and resting my head against his chest after removing my glasses and setting them on the nightstand. My sleep mask is on and resting on my forehead for now. He strokes my hair and kisses the top of my head.

"Night, little rabbit," he coos in my ear.

"Night," I reply and pull my mask over my eyes before I drift to sleep.

PARKER

I wake before Rory the next morning. He fell asleep against me last night, but we moved around a bit and I ended up spooning him. I drink in his pumpkin and nutmeg scent as I slip my hand under his shirt, which has ridden up considerably in his sleep and is now bunched up just above his panties. I trace my fingers over his flat belly and along his abdomen, and he squirms. I lean in and nibble on his ear, making him shudder.

"Morning, cutie pie." He moans and presses his tushy against my crotch, rubbing against my rapidly hardening dick.

"More," he whines. Christ on a cracker. I can't believe anyone ever thought he was anything but a fucking dream in bed, because I can't get enough of his sweet noises and neediness. I'm so honored that he wants to share this part of himself with me, and I will always make sure he knows how perfect he is. I love seeing my marks on his body; his neck, shoulder and belly, and it just makes me want him all over again.

I lick at the spots on his neck and shoulder where I left marks yesterday, then suck and bite, leaving a few new ones as he moans and gasps, his perky little ass pushing against me again and again, making me harder and harder. "You taste amazing, little rabbit," I tell him. "Look so good covered in my marks."

"Parker," he moans, bringing his arm up and gripping the back of my neck. I trace my fingers around his belly button and then bite down lightly on his earlobe, and he shudders, bucking his hips forward. Then he's rolling over and shoving me on my back before he straddles me. The T-shirt of mine he's wearing is pooled around his thighs as he sits on top of me and I grin at the sight of his nasal strip across his nose, his kitty cat mask on his forehead, and his mussed up curls. But the best part is the fact that he's hard and his cute little dick is tenting the T-shirt. He's the cutest thing on the planet.

"Stop teasing me," he says, and I grin wider as he grips my arms and holds them above my head. I could fight him and break out of his grip in an instant if I wanted to, but I don't. He looks adorable when he's grumpy and horny and trying to be all tough. He ruts against me and I can't help the groan that escapes my lips. The slide of his cock against mine is sending bolts of pleasure racing up my spine. He bends down to kiss me, letting go of my wrists as he does, and I grip his curls in my hands as our tongues tangle and we continue to gyrate.

"Fuck," he says, pulling back. "Get naked."

I grin wider and he climbs off of me, stripping out of the T-shirt and panties and tossing them aside. I love his confidence, hearing him give orders, knowing what he wants and asking for it. It's so hot. I strip out of my pajama pants and briefs and then he's on top of me again. "Oh, fuck," I moan as I grip his hips and feel his naked cock sliding against mine. "You feel so good, freckles."

His dick twitches at my words and he smiles, leaning down to kiss me again. Every inch of his warm soft skin feels incredible as it brushes against me. My cock is leaking all over my belly as he kisses me and moves his torso so his stomach and chest brush against mine, making my entire body shudder. I grunt and reach between us, taking both of our cocks in my hand, and Rory pulls back with a gasp when I stroke us together.

"Holy fuck." He plants his hands on either side of my head and looks down at where I'm gripping us. I stroke again, using our precum as lube. His head falls back on a moan that borders on pornographic and it makes me even more desperate to get him off, to get us both off, together. "Nnnn, shit, that's good." He sits up, his hands resting on my chest as he juts his cock out, thrusting into my palm. The slide of his dick against mine makes me groan and grip us harder.

"God, you're sexy," I tell him.

"Oh, fuck, Parker, this…this feels so good. God, don't stop."

"Your cock is amazing, little rabbit," I tell him, my breaths heavier and my voice husky. His dick jumps in my grip and it's so fucking hot I almost come right then. I can't stop staring at him, his head thrown back, mouth parted in bliss, his body damp with sweat and my marks covering his small frame.

When he brings his hands up and starts playing with his own nipples, I fucking lose it. "Shit, that's hot," I groan. "I'm gonna come watching you, freckles. You're so fucking pretty."

He doesn't stop, and I stroke us two more times before I'm arching my back and spraying all over my hand and both of our cocks. I use my jizz as lube and stroke Rory again. He looks down and his body shudders. "Oh, shit, that's hot," he says. Then a second later, "Oh, oh, oh, fuck, I'm coming, fuck, Parker, I'm coming!" He throws his head back again, his abdominal muscles tightening as he shouts his release. Then he's collapsing on top of me, and we're both breathing heavily. His body spasms with the aftershocks of his orgasm.

"That was amazing," he says, his cheek resting against my chest.

I comb my fingers through his hair. "Mmmm," I murmur, then ask, "Have you never frotted before?"

He looks up at me, his cheeks pink with embarrassment as he bites his lip. "Is that what it's called? Rubbing our dicks together?"

I nod and he shakes his head. My eyes narrow. "I'm sorry," he says. His eyes fill with tears.

"Hey, no," I tell him, quickly. A tear slides down his cheek and it breaks my heart. "You don't have anything to be sorry for. I'm honored to be the person who experienced that with you for the first time, little rabbit. I just hate that turd for not sharing it with you a long time ago, too."

He nods and wipes at his cheeks. "He wasn't really big on making sex about me, or even us. It was kind of about him. I blew him, and I bottomed for him. Occasionally he'd blow me, but he always made a big deal about how much I should appreciate it because it wasn't his favorite, and that was about it. And I really didn't like bottoming either. It hurt too much. I just did it to make him happy."

I take a breath in and let it out. "If he was taking care of you it shouldn't have hurt, at least not the entire time. Bottoming is really amazing if you do it right. I'm sorry he didn't treat you the way you deserved."

"Yeah, me, too," he says, offering a small smile.

"You don't ever have to do something you don't want to do, with me," I assure him. "I want to make you feel good, little rabbit. If you aren't having a good time, I'm not either."

He smiles more at that. "Thank you." Then he lays back

down and I drape my arms over him, holding him against me.

"We should get cleaned up," I tell him a moment later as I stroke my fingers up and down his spine.

He picks his head up again. "What time is it?"

I reach for my phone on the nightstand and say, "Nine thirty."

He grabs the phone and his eyes widen. "Shit." He jumps off of me and rushes towards the bathroom. "I have class at ten." Oops. I wipe the majority of our cum off with the tissues next to me. He's in and out of the shower in five minutes and running out of my room and down the hall, his towel around his waist.

I slide out of bed and pee, before I wash my hands. I'm still in the bathroom when he bursts back in the room, dressed in blue slim fitting pants, a white button up shirt with blue polka dots on it and a blue bow tie. His suspenders are brown as are his shoes, and he looks so fucking cute. He grabs his glasses from the nightstand and slips them on, then hurries over to me and presses up on his tiptoes, planting a kiss on my cheek. "Bye," he calls, before dashing away again. I chuckle when I hear the front door closing behind him.

ELEVEN

PARKER

Rory and I fuck like rabbits for the next couple of weeks. My little roomie comes alive in the sheets. He's passionate, eager, energetic, and makes the sexiest noises that have me so fucking hard each and every time.

We've stuck to non penetrative sex so far, hand jobs, blow jobs, frotting, which the little dude is obsessed with now, and dry humping, and it's been awesome seeing him come out of his shell and enjoy sex in a way I don't think he has before. He sleeps in my room most nights, and we cuddle. He loves being the little spoon, and we both sleep better when we're together. He's getting more and more dominant in bed, and I don't mind one bit. He tells me what he likes, and is more often than not the one instigating our sexual encounters, and the little dude is amazing at blow jobs.

I've also noticed he wears his pretty panties pretty much every day now, and it makes me smile. I can't get enough of seeing him in them. His confidence is growing and I love it. And ever since he blocked Zach's number he's been happier. Smiling more, laughing more. He has the most adorable laugh, and when he gets going really hard he snorts a little and it's the cutest thing ever.

Rory is on the phone with someone when I get back from classes and I can tell he's a little nervous from the way he's picking at his sweater and fidgeting with the pen on the counter.

"Yeah, okay, I'll figure out something. Thank you." He hangs up and sets his phone on the counter, then gives me a timid smile. I set my backpack down on the sofa and move over to him, pressing a kiss to his cheek.

"Everything okay?" I ask. He grips his sleeves and shoves his hands inside, then pushes his glasses up on his nose even though they haven't moved.

"Yeah, it's fine. Just a little hiccup with a doctor's appointment I have to figure out."

"What is it?" I ask, rubbing his back. I've noticed how the right touch soothes him when he's upset or anxious. Stroking his hair, rubbing his back or his feet. He lets out a breath and his shoulders loosen a bit.

"I had an endoscopy scheduled for when I went back home for Thanksgiving break, and one of my parents was going to take me, but the doctor's office called and they have to move the appointment up, and they changed the location to closer to here, though it's still like a forty minute drive, and I'm trying to figure out how to get there because I have to have someone drive me home."

"When is it?" I ask.

"Next week. Tuesday morning. I can't ask Jackson and Lucy because they're both going home for Thanksgiving on Saturday. I was going to go too, but now I have to stay until after the procedure."

I bite my lip. "You could ask me. I don't know when I am leaving yet but I can take you first."

His eyes widen and he flushes, pushing his glasses up on his nose yet again. "Oh, no, you don't need to do that. I mean,

I couldn't ask you. It's a lot of driving and sitting there for hours waiting and I don't want you to be uncomfortable."

I shrug. "I don't mind. I could get some homework done while I waited and I don't have anywhere else to be."

Rory bites his lip. "Really? I mean, that would be amazing, and I could pay you for gas and everything. Well, my parents would pay you. But I really don't want you to feel like you have to just because we're...um." He flushes even more and motions between us, "you know."

I grin and ruffle his hair. "I'm not taking you because we're getting freaky in the sheets, freckles. I'm taking you because you need someone and I'm your friend. Right?"

A smile breaks out across his face and he nods. "Yeah."

"Okay, then, it's settled." I grab a banana and peel it open, taking a bite as I settle on the sofa and pull my laptop out of my bag.

"Hey, what do you think of having a gathering with our friends this weekend? Friday night?" Rory says from his spot at the bar, turning to face me. "I haven't seen Lucy and Jackson in a while."

"A gathering?" I tease him. "You mean a party?"

He flushes again. "Gathering sounds calmer."

I chuckle. "Gathering it is." Then more seriously I say, "Can you handle that many people at once?"

"Yeah, if we aren't playing super loud music or having the tv up really loud I can. I'll wear my earplugs. It should be okay for a couple of hours."

"Okay," I say. "Let me know if you need me to shove people out." I text my friends, and they all reply within a couple of minutes saying they'll be there. When I look up, Rory is smiling at his phone.

"Good?" I say, and he nods.

"They're coming." He waits a beat and I'm back to working on my homework when he speaks again, softer this time. "Do you think you could make your chocolate chip cookies? For the party, I mean? I told Jackson and Lucy how good they are and they really want to try them."

I grin. "Sure. Anything for you, little rabbit." His cheeks pinken even more and he grins at me. We work on homework for a couple more hours before we break for dinner.

We're watching an episode of *The Big Bang Theory* when Rory moves his head from my shoulder and starts licking and sucking on my earlobe. I close my eyes and moan as my cock hardens in an instant.

"Oh, Jesus, freckles," I murmur, squirming and adjusting myself. "You know I'm a sucker for that."

He giggles and it makes me even harder. He continues to suck and nibble before whispering, "Want you, big boy. Come and get me."

Holy cookie crumbles. I love when he's like this. Demanding, horny, sexy as fuck. I turn and slot my lips against his, wrapping my arms around him and drawing him to me. He gasps and I feel my cock jerking as I hold him to me and suck on his tongue, him practically in my lap now. I feel his dick against my stomach and my cock throbs in my jeans as he whimpers and whines into the kiss, my hands skating up his sweater and along his spine.

"Mmmmnnngg," he moans, pulling away and rutting against me. "More."

I almost growl and kiss him harder. "Fuck, little rabbit, you make me so hard." He sits back and starts to undress and I do the same.

"You okay with trying something new?" I ask him as I shuck off my boxers and they join the rest of my clothes on the floor.

He nods, tossing his pants on the floor, leaving him in just a plain black g-string that has my cock spasming and precum leaking out in droves. I grab my dick and squeeze it as I stare at him. "Fuuuck," I rumble, drawing the word out. He blushes and bites his lip. Then he's straddling me and I groan when I feel his hard dick through the thong, brushing up against mine, his bare skin sending waves of pleasure through my body as I hold him close and kiss him fiercely. My hands are everywhere and it's not enough. I'm still kissing him as I lower him onto his back and hover over him. I moan as our tongues tangle and he lets out the sexiest whimpers and bucks his hips up into me, seeking friction. God, I'm so damn hard, my cock leaking onto his belly as he runs his fingers through my hair and grips my cock, stroking it. I jerk at the sensation and slide my tongue a little further into his mouth. He tastes like lemon and pepper from the meal we had, and his hand feels incredible on my cock. A little too incredible.

"I need you on your hands and knees," I tell him, my voice raspy when I pull away. He releases my dick and raises an eyebrow. "I won't use my cock," I promise. He nods and rolls over. "Top half down," I instruct and he lowers his head and torso so that his cute as hell ass is in the air and I see the thin strip of material from his thong between his ass cheeks. My mouth waters. "Damn." I grip his cheeks and massage them and he moans. Then I'm burying my face in his ass crack and breathing in. He jerks and gasps.

"Oh," he breathes, and a shiver races through him before he wiggles his ass. I breathe in again before I nibble and suck on the right cheek. He lets out another gasp and then a series of moans and whimpers as I continue to lavish his adorable tushy with kisses, licks and nibbles, moving from one cheek to the other. "Oh, fuck, Parker. Oh, oh, mmmnnngg, fuck, fuck."

"Fucking cheese puffs I can't get enough of you," I tell him. I bite down on his ass cheek, sucking, marking him, making him squeak and jerk slightly before I lick a strip from his taint to his hole. He shakes and gasps again.

"Oh, fuck."

"This okay?" I ask, and he nods vigorously. His thong is still there and I move it out of the way before I repeat the motion, slowly. I hum when my tongue glides up his naked skin and then lick his hole a few times, savoring the taste of him. His body shudders and he moans, lifting his head slightly and pushing his ass back, begging for more.

Yes.

"Fuck, that's good," he whines. Sweat glistens on pale skin and his cheeks are flushed. He looks so perfect like this.

"You taste amazing, little rabbit," I tell him, then return to my task. He bucks his hips as I lick and suck and nibble on his gorgeous little pucker, shockwaves of pleasure racing down my spine each time, and making my balls draw up. I want to touch myself so badly but I want him more, and I need to use my hands to keep his cheeks spread.

He whimpers, and I see the goosebumps breaking out along his skin. "Fuck, I'm close, Parker," he tells me, and his voice breaks when he says my name. I hum and go for the gold. I slide my tongue inside him and he mewls, his body shaking and his hips thrusting frantically as I eat him out.

"Oh, god, oh fuck, oh fuck, oh, oh, so good, Parker. Oh god, I'm coming." I feel his ass clenching around my tongue as he comes hard, and then I'm sliding out and stroking myself hard and fast, my cock hard as granite, the tip red and angry, aching for relief.

"Stay there," I manage to get out as Rory pants, his cheek resting on his arms. I stroke myself two times and then I'm howling as I spray my release all over his crack and ass cheeks. I'm so fucking turned on by the sight that my cock jerks and a second shot of cum shoots out to join the first.

He trembles, looking back at me and his ass. "Fuck. That was hot."

I nod, watching as my cum slides between his legs and down his thighs. "Jesus, that's pretty."

He flushes and says, "Give me some."

My eyes widen and I swipe some of my release from his thigh onto my finger and lean forward, putting it near his lips. He grabs my finger and his tongue darts out, licking the cum from it and swallowing it down greedily.

"Holy hell," I murmur.

He grins.

RORY

"Who did you say is taking you to the endoscopy?" Mom asks me when I'm Facetiming her the next day.

"My roommate, Parker."

She frowns. "I thought Zach was your roommate."

"Yeah, he was, but he isn't now. We broke up." I haven't said anything about Zach cheating on me or about moving in with Parker and I know I waited way too long, but I couldn't bring myself to tell her before now. Everything was too raw and fresh and I just needed some time to adjust.

"Oh. I'm sorry, honey. Are you okay?"

"Yeah, I am now," I tell her, and can't help the smile that spreads across my face.

"I see," she says. "Parker must be a great guy."

I'm blushing furiously and really wishing we'd just done a regular phone call, but she said she wanted to see my face, and my sisters did too.

"Hey, kiddo," Dad says, shoving his face into the screen. Mom shoves him away playfully and I laugh when he kisses her cheek, then slides his glasses back up on his nose. I look like him, with the curly brown hair and freckles, though he's several inches taller than me. I get my height from Mom. She's short and stout. Her brown hair is wavy and falls to her shoulders and her eyes are warm.

"Hi, Dad."

"How are classes?" he calls from the background now.

"Good," I say, chuckling slightly. He knows Mom is front and center whenever we talk and he's lucky to get any screen time at all.

"He has a new roommate," Mom pipes up. "Parker."

"What happened to Zach?" Dad asks her, like I'm not right there.

"Broke up. He's okay, though."

"Oh, good. Sorry we never got to meet him."

"Don't be," I say with a sigh.

"So now that I know you're okay," Mom says, her voice a bit more stern. "When were you going to tell me you moved, and what are you doing with the money I'm sending you every month to pay rent and buy groceries? Is it the same amount? Do you need more? You're eating well, I hope. You look thin."

"I'm fine," I groan. "I don't need any more money. Rent is a little bit cheaper, actually. I'm sorry I didn't tell you sooner. It was rough for a while."

"Breakups are never easy," she says. "But it sounds like you did the right thing. I'm proud of you."

"Me, too!" Dad shouts from somewhere off screen, and I chuckle.

"Thanks," I reply. "And thanks for not being super mad at me for keeping it a secret."

"Oh, you can pay me back by taking pictures of the apartment I'm paying for," she says, smiling, though I know she's serious.

"Yeah, sure. As soon as I get off the phone."

"And I want to hear more about this Parker some time. He sounds nice. Tell him thank you from us for taking my baby to surgery. You feel safe, comfortable with him doing that? You sure you don't want your dad or me to come?"

I shake my head. "It's like the tenth one I've had, you know that. I'll be fine. Just routine at this point. And it's a long drive for you guys to make. And honestly, I think he really wants to do it. He's super sweet and he likes taking care of me." I flush when the words are out of my mouth, not sure why I said all of that, but it's true. And it's how I feel. I'm feeling a lot of things towards Parker that I've never felt for anyone before.

"Oh, okay," Mom says, her eyes twinkling, and I can tell she's thinking something she won't share. "Give Parker our number so he can text or call when you're at your appointment and tell us how you're doing."

"Yeah, okay."

"Who's Parker?" I hear and then the face on the phone changes to Ava's and I hear Mom scoffing.

"Young lady, you know better than to snatch something out of someone's hand. Give it back, please, and ask nicely."

Ava sighs and I chuckle, before I see Mom's face again and then Ava next to her this time. "Can I please have the phone?" She says it like she's twelve and not seven, just enough attitude to skate by without getting punished.

Then I'm looking at her again and this time Addison is there too. I smile at my sisters. Addison waves but doesn't say anything. She's the more timid of the two. I wave back, resting against my headboard.

"You guys behaving?" I ask.

Ava waves a finger at me. "No way, don't change the subject," she says. "I know you heard me. Who's Parker?"

"His boyfriend!" Dad shouts and I feel my cheeks heating. Addison gasps, her face lighting up. Ava purses her lips.

"I thought Zach was your boyfriend," she says.

"They broke up!" Dad shouts again, and I groan, covering my face with my hand.

Ava gasps now. "Did he hurt you?" She scowls into the phone and I can't help laughing. She seriously would go after Zach if I let her. She'd probably win, too.

"It's fine," I tell her. "And Parker isn't my boyfriend. We're just roommates."

"I want to meet him. He better be treating you right."

I flush. "He treats me just fine."

"You tell me if he doesn't." She points her finger at me.

"Yes, Ma'am," I say with a solute. She grins and then proceeds to tell me all about her day. The boy she has a crush on, the kid in her class who got in trouble for swearing, and the fact that her and Addison are graduating to green belts in their karate class in December and since I'll be home for Christmas break I'll get to see it.

"Can't wait," I tell her. "Hey, let me talk to Addy for a bit. Love you, sis."

"Love you, too," she says.

"Hey, princess," I say when Addison is holding the phone.

"Hi," she says. Her voice is soft but she's smiling. It turns to a frown when she says, "I miss you."

My heart squeezes. "I miss you too, Addy Bear. I'll be home for Thanksgiving soon, okay? We can have a tea party and you can introduce me to your new plushies."

She grins. "Okay. I have a new crown, too. You can wear it if you want."

I smile widely. "I would love to. You enjoying karate still?"

She nods.

"You gonna get a black belt and kick everyone's butts?" I ask, and she giggles.

"Rory Campbell," I hear Mom's voice and Addison giggles again. "We don't encourage violence, young man. You know that. Karate is for self defense. Not kicking butts."

Addison and I both chuckle and I wink at her. "I should go," I tell her. "Love you."

"Love you, too," she says, and I hang up. I set my phone down and lie back on my bed, staring up at the ceiling as I run my fingers through my hair and bite my lip.

Would Parker be my boyfriend if I asked him? Should I ask him? We've been having a lot of sex and it's been amazing. Better than I ever dreamed sex could be, but I can't help wanting more. He's the best person I know and he makes me happy, makes me better. He gave me the courage to break ties with Zach, to stand up for myself. I feel more confident because of him. I don't think I'm scared of making a mistake with him anymore. I know who he is. He's genuine, and kind, and he's the same person with me that he is with my friends.

He always puts me first and makes sure I'm comfortable and safe in bed. Zach never did that.

No, I'm not afraid of finding out he's different. I'm afraid of him rejecting me when I finally muster up the courage to ask for more. To define what we are and what we're doing. I want more than just sex with him. I have since I moved in and realized what an amazing guy he is. But what if he doesn't want the same thing?

I sigh and roll off the bed, heading down the hall and into the living area where Parker is talking on the phone. He grins at me and goes back to talking.

"No, it's fine. Yeah, I'm sure. Don't worry about it. I'll be okay. I know. Mom, I know. It's fine. Please don't cry, Mom. I promise I'll be okay. I'll see you guys at Christmas. Okay. I love you, too."

He hangs up and gives me another small smile as he shoves his phone in his pocket.

"What was that about?" I ask. "I mean, if you want to tell me, that is. Because of course you don't have to. You just, I mean, it sounded, um, I mean. Is anything wrong?" Parker crosses the room as I ramble and then he's kissing me. I melt into the kiss and he's smiling again when he pulls away. "Is something wrong?" I ask again.

"No, not really," he tells me. "Just not going home for Thanksgiving, but it's fine."

I frown. "Oh. How come?"

He flushes.

"Shit. Sorry. I'm being really nosy. I don't mean to be, I just want to help."

"I know, freckles," he says. Then presses another kiss to my nose. "Things are tight right now, for them. They can't afford to bring me home this year and then pay for me to come home at Christmas too. It's okay, though. It's just a few more weeks until Christmas. It'll be fine. Mom was just emotional. She feels bad."

"Oh, I'm sorry." I hate that Parker can't be with his family over the Thanksgiving break, and I hate even more the thought of him being here all alone.

"There's gotta be other students who aren't going home. I'll find someone to hang out with." He gives me a grin and then moves towards the kitchen.

"What if you came home with me?" I ask, the words flying out of my mouth before I can stop myself.

He turns to me, hazel eyes wide. "Really?"

I flush. "Yeah, I mean, it's about a two hour drive, and you'll be stuck in the car with me the entire time, but I'm sure my parents would be happy to have you. They wanted to say thank you for taking me to my endoscopy anyway, so this is perfect. They'll talk your ear off and my sisters will cajole you into playing dress up, but if you're okay with that…" I trail off, fidgeting with my suspenders.

He grins. "That'd be awesome."

I can't help it. I beam at him. "Great. I'll text them. Oh, and they wanted you to have their number so you can update them during the procedure and afterwards."

"Of course," he says. I text my parents, letting them know I'm bringing Parker home for Thanksgiving, and Mom immediately replies telling me how wonderful that is and that they can't wait to meet him. Then I text their number to Parker. He immediately starts typing on his phone and then a moment later it dings.

"Ahh, your mom is so sweet," he says, typing again. "She just said thanks for taking care of her baby boy." He talks as he types out the message I'm assuming he's sending back to her. **"No problem, Mrs. C. Rory is the best."**

"Oh, god," I groan. "This was a mistake. A horrible, horrible mistake."

He looks at me, a frown on his face, his eyes so sad I feel a pain in my chest. "You don't want me to come anymore?"

My eyes widen. "No," I say. "I mean, yes. I mean, I was just joking. Of course I want you to come home with me. I was being sarcastic, like I was terrified of you talking to my mom, but it's fine."

He grins and goes back to typing. Jesus, that look on his face. I forget that Parker doesn't understand sarcasm sometimes. But, oh boy. Mom and Parker messaging each other can't be good.

"Ahh, she just asked if there was anything in particular I want for Thanksgiving dinner," Parker croons when his phone pings again. "What do you guys usually have?"

"Uh, I don't know. Turkey, mashed potatoes, salad, deviled eggs, stuffing, rolls, green bean casserole."

"That all sounds good to me." He types back and presses send. Then he's laughing when his phone pings again and he reads Mom's reply to whatever he sent her.

Lord, I think Mom and Parker are going to be best friends before they even meet.

TWELVE

RORY

Two days later, I'm at the campus bookstore again for my middle of the day shift. Tonight is our gathering with our friends and I'm really looking forward to it, but I have another hour here before I can head home and start getting ready.

It's not super busy but there are a few people milling around while I sit behind the counter, reading.

I've got my head down when I hear a familiar voice. "Hey, Rory. Your guard dog isn't here huh? He let you out of the house by yourself? I thought you were his little bitch. Or is it the other way around?"

My cheeks flush. I tense slightly, but not like I used to when Zach harassed me. I'm calmer, though my heart rate is picking up a little bit. But I don't feel as upset, or scared. His words don't matter anymore. I know the things he says aren't about me. They're about him. No, this time, I'm not letting him treat me like this. I ignore him and hear a snarl.

"Can I help you?" I ask, looking up. He narrows his eyes at me. "Don't you have a boy toy to go stick your dick in?" Woah, I can't believe I just said that, but Zach's cheeks are reddening and I have to admit it's kinda satisfying. "Or did they all get tired of your narcissistic bullshit too?"

He glares, his cheeks getting even redder. "You little bitch," he snarls in a whisper, fists clenched at his side.

"Say whatever you want, but I'm done letting you upset me," I tell him. My heart rate is picking up but I don't stop. "You're a bully and an asshole who's so insecure he tears other people down to make himself feel better. And I let you belittle me, and hurt me for a long time, but not anymore. I know who I am. I like who I am. And your words are just noise. So fuck off."

His eyes widen. He stares at me for a moment, like he can't believe what he heard. "You're such a fucking loser, Rory," he tells me finally, before he turns and stalks away.

"Woah," Parker says, when I tell him about my run in with Zach later that day. "Are you okay?"

"Yeah," I say, and I find that I'm actually smiling. I was shaking a little bit after he left, but that's worn off now. "I mean, it honestly felt really good to tell him how I felt."

Parker grins at me, then kisses my forehead. He's frowning though, when he pulls away. "Are you safe?" he asks. "I mean, he wouldn't hurt you, would he?"

I shake my head. "No, he's an asshole but he isn't violent. I don't think I have to worry about him anymore."

Parker grins again. "I'm proud of you."

I smile wider. "I'm proud of me, too."

I've got the main lights turned off and the living area illuminated by lamps only. It helps with me not getting overstimulated, and honestly I think it works better for the vibe.

We've got snacks set up on the bar and drinks in the

refrigerator. Everyone showed up, but Lucy and I were exchanging looks when Jackson and Preston arrived together. They told us they ran into each other in the hallway on the way up here, but they both look a bit flushed, and Jackson's hair is messier than I've ever seen it.

I think back to when Parker and I saw the two of them at the Halloween party, and then a couple of weeks ago when Jackson was hanging out with Lucy and me, and left in the middle of the movie we were watching because he had "somewhere he had to be." At midnight.

"Are they....?" I ask her as we stand in the kitchen sipping our drinks. I mentioned the situation with Zach to her too, and she beamed with pride.

I have a soda and Lucy has sparkling water. I think the stuff is nasty but she loves it so I always have some for her when she comes over.

She shrugs. "He hasn't told me anything. But, I have a feeling something is going on between them. He's been secretive lately, texting someone and then hurrying off. Remember a couple weeks ago?" I nod.

"More of that stuff. We were hanging out the other day at my place and he just up and told me he had to leave out of nowhere and then scurried away like his pants were on fire. He's been acting weird since the Halloween party."

I raise an eyebrow and we both look in Jackson's direction. He's in the living room, laughing with Parker at the moment, but Preston is nearby, and the way he looks at my friend tells me he's either getting some, or wishes he was. "They were kinda friendly that night, remember?" I say. "Parker and I saw them."

She hums. "Speaking of bed partners," she says, a grin growing on her face. Oh, no. "Have you and Parker....?"

My cheeks heat. "Ahhh!!" She squeals, "I knew it."

"Shhh," I hush her, and she laughs. "Jesus, I don't need the entire apartment building knowing."

"Sorry," she says. "I'm just super happy for you. He's a really great guy."

"I know," I say, my gaze straying back to him. He's got all of his friends and Jackson laughing now at something, and they're slapping his back.

"Oh, honey," Lucy says, "you've got it bad."

I sigh and take another sip of my drink as I watch Parker take a seat on the couch and pick up a *Nintendo Switch* controller. Chris sits next to him and then I hear him say, "Get ready to cry, mother fucker." Then, "Winner keeps playing. Loser hands the controller to the next person."

"I know."

"Does he know you want more?"

I shake my head.

"Why haven't you told him?"

"It's too soon," I say. "I don't want to scare him off. And I know I'm not the easiest person to date."

She frowns. "That's your idiot ex getting in your head again. Jesus, I hate that he made you feel that way about yourself. The right person isn't going to make you feel like you owe them for being in a relationship with you. I've seen the way Parker looks at you, babe. And he's taking you to get an endoscopy, and didn't you tell me he took you to get your blood drawn?"

I nod, biting my lip.

"That doesn't sound like someone who is upset or overwhelmed by making sure you're taken care of. He's crazy about you, Rory. I don't think there's anything you could do that would scare him off."

She snatches her third chocolate chip cookie and takes a huge bite, then grins at me. "Besides, he makes cookies better than my grandma, so he's definitely a keeper."

I smile, and she winks at me, before we head into the living room to join the others.

It's not until after I've finished my turn playing against Parker in Mario Kart, and losing epically, that I realize

Preston and Jackson are nowhere in sight. And thank god for my earplugs, because I never realized a game of Mario Kart could be so loud. I'm managing so far, but I'm guessing I have about another thirty minutes in me before I need to kick people out. I figure I can get a break in the bathroom and pee, so I make my way down the hall, only to stop when I hear raised voices from the other side of the door.

"I'm sorry, I just, it's hard, okay?" Preston's voice.

"Look, this is why I didn't want to come. It was risky enough showing up here together, and I don't think Lucy and Rory bought for a second that we ran into each other on the way up. You can't be touching me, or fucking looking at me like that, not here. Not in front of them. Or they'll definitely know something is up."

"It would have been riskier to both not come. How do you think that would look? I don't understand why it's such a big deal anyway, if they know." Preston sounds absolutely crestfallen.

"Because we agreed it would just be casual. Hooking up. That's it. I don't need it announced."

There's silence before Preston speaks again. "Fine. I'll leave. That will make it easier. Then you can enjoy the evening without worrying about me."

Fuck. I scramble across the hall to my room and shut the door before I hear the bathroom door opening.

"Preston, wait, I didn't…" I hear Jackson saying, and footsteps moving down the hall.

Holy shit.

The weekend passes and before I know it, it's the day of my endoscopy. It's nothing new to me. I've been having them since I was a kid, so I'm not nervous about the procedure itself, just the IV that they'll give me beforehand. The procedure only takes about ten minutes, and they put you to sleep.

Then I'll be home the same day and might have a bit of a sore throat, but other than that I'll just be groggy from the anesthesia. I started a different medication a few months back, right before I met Parker, and the doctor wants to see how it's working, so they'll take a look inside and check my esophagus and stomach for anything abnormal or anything that would indicate the medication is not working.

"Ready?" Parker says, poking his head in my room. Ever since we started sleeping together I don't close the door anymore when I change unless there's someone else in the apartment. I'm wearing a pair of sweats and a loose fitting T-shirt, so that I'm comfortable. I'm also fucking starving because I haven't been able to have anything but clear liquid since noon the day before.

"Yeah," I tell him. We grab our coats off the hooks by the front door and slide our shoes on, then make our way through the snow to Parker's car. It's been a bit since we had fresh snow, but there's a few inches of it covering the grass, and although the sun is shining there's a bit of a breeze this morning, and the winter chill bites at my face as I crunch through the parking lot. I shiver once I'm in the car, and Parker turns on the defroster before pulling out of the parking lot.

It's about a forty minute drive, and I spend the first ten shivering until the heat finally warms up enough.

Parker chuckles. "You still cold?"

"I'm always cold," I tell him. He has his coat, which isn't anywhere near as thick as mine, unzipped, and he has all of the air vents aimed at me. "Shit, are you hot?"

"Nah, it's fine. I don't want you to be cold."

God, this guy. Always putting me first. It's overwhelming sometimes, and there are times where I don't feel like I deserve it, or wonder if he can even be real because he's just too damn amazing and he makes me feel more worthy and beautiful than I ever have before.

I'm picturing us making the trip to my parents' house for

Thanksgiving with him in shorts and a T-shirt so he doesn't get too hot, and me in layers so I don't get too cold, and it makes me chuckle. I start laughing harder until I snort, then cover my nose and mouth with my hand, my cheeks heating. He just looks at me with a grin and says, "I love your laugh."

He tells me to play some music and I turn on Taylor Swift, then start singing along and dancing as much as one can in their seat and he grins at me again. "You're too stinkin cute," he says, and I smile. I flush when he reaches over and takes my hand, making my body erupt in goosebumps. Fuck, why is that simple act making my brain short circuit? We've held hands before when we're sitting on the sofa watching tv, but this feels different. He squeezes my hand.

"This okay?" he asks, and I nod, unable to form words. "I really like you," he says after a moment of silence. "I just want you to know that."

I swallow. I've never had anyone say that to me before. It feels amazing, and the fact that I know I can trust him, that he treats me well, that he cares for me, and has never done anything to hurt me or take advantage of me, makes it mean even more. My chest squeezes and I have to keep the tears from filling my eyes. It takes me a moment to form words, but I squeeze his hand and say, "I really like you, too."

His smile is the most beautiful thing I've ever seen.

PARKER

I'm still holding Rory's hand when we arrive at the surgery center forty minutes later. I do have to let go in order to park and get out but I slide my hand right back in his as we're making our way through the parking lot and along the sidewalk to the front door. We take the elevator up to the second floor and go inside. There's a small waiting room with several people already here, and I have a feeling we might be waiting a while.

Rory signs in and we take our seats. He texts his mom to let her know we're here and then his hand is finding mine again, and I grin. I was going to do some homework on my laptop, but since my hand is occupied I decide to scroll through social media for a bit instead, and he does the same. We share funny videos and memes with each other and then Rory starts reading something on his phone.

After another half an hour they finally call Rory's name, and he stands with his hand still clasping mine.

"Can my friend come?" he asks, and I feel his palm sweating and the tremor that moves through his body. Poor little dude. He is so terrified of getting the IV I'm afraid he'll hyperventilate or something.

"Sure," the nurse, a small Asian American woman says, and waves us back. She leads us to a curtained off area with patients on both sides and tells Rory to sit on the bed while I take a seat in the chair nearby. There's so little room I have to try and make myself as small as possible. They instruct him to change into the hospital gown they have laid out on the bed and he strips out of his T-shirt and slides it on, shoving his shirt, shoes, phone, and glasses into a bag and handing it to me. When the nurse returns she asks him a million questions about his health history, and he doesn't seem to mind answering them in front of me. I'm surprised to find I know most of it already. She tells him they'll get the IV going when she's finished with all of his information and he murmurs, "Yay, my favorite part."

I raise an eyebrow. "I thought you hated needles. You're shaking like a leaf."

He looks at me and blinks, then squeezes my hand. "I am," he says. "I was joking."

"Oh." My cheeks heat. "Right. I knew that."

He chuckles and at least my ignorance gave him a reason to laugh, so I'll take it.

"You're afraid of needles?" the nurse asks. Rory nods, and she says she'll take good care of him and recline the bed so he doesn't pass out.

His hand is still gripping mine when he's reclined and all the questions have been answered, and I squeeze again. His face has gone slightly pale and I use my other hand to stroke his arm, trying to soothe him as best I can.

"You're okay," I tell him as the nurse preps him for the IV. "You're going to do just fine."

He nods, taking a deep breath and letting it out. He makes a fist with his hand when he's told to and hisses slightly when the nurse applies the tourniquet.

"You okay?" she asks, with a soft smile and kind eyes as she moves her finger along his arm, tapping, searching for a vein.

Rory nods but he's trembling.

"Hey, look at me," I tell him. He does. "You got this. You're so brave, little dude."

"Okay, here we go," the nurse tells him. I squeeze his hand and feel his body tensing and another hiss leaving his lips, but he does it.

"It's in," the nurse says. "Worst part is over. You did really well, sweetie." She tapes it on the inside of his elbow and tosses everything in the trash.

Rory closes his eyes for a minute, his hand tight around mine. It's several more moments before he relaxes and looks at me.

"Thank you," he says, his voice soft. "I'm really glad you're here."

"Me, too," I say.

It's a while later that the doctor and the anesthesiologist come by to talk to him, and a while after that before the nurse comes by again and tells me it's time for me to head out to the waiting room and that they'll let me know when Rory is awake and ready to go home.

I nod and stand, pressing a kiss to his forehead before I

walk away. I've been texting Rory's mom this whole time, letting her know he's been doing fine. I update her once I'm back in the waiting room, and she thanks me profusely for the millionth time for looking out for her baby boy.

Rory is finished not long after that and I can't help chuckling when I drive around to pick him up, and he's so loopy that nothing he's saying makes sense. He repeats himself half a dozen times, saying something about cats and rainbows before moving on to one word.

"Food," he says. Then repeats it when I ask him where he wants to eat.

"I can make you something," I say. "Or I can pick something up after I drop you off at home."

He licks his lips and then hiccups loudly, and I chuckle again.

"Ow," he groans. Then hiccups again.

Since he hasn't answered my question yet, I ask again. He looks at me like he isn't sure who I am, blinking several times as he stares. "I'm hungry. And thirsty."

"I know," I tell him. "What do you want?"

He looks like he's considering it, then says, "Food," again. "I'm hungry. And tired. They never give you enough time to sleep after those procedures, you know? They're practically slapping you awake and yelling at you to get the fuck up and get dressed already. Not nice." He yawns. "I'm tired."

"Twenty more minutes. You can sleep now if you want."

"Oh, good," he says, resting his head back against the seat. "Cuz I'm tired."

I look over a few minutes later to see him asleep, his mouth hanging open and a small bit of drool sliding down his chin.

When I park the car in the apartment parking lot twenty minutes later, he's still passed out, so I climb out and go around to his side. I open the door and scoop him up, holding him to me and closing the door with my hip before carrying him inside. I struggle a bit, trying to figure out how to get inside with him in my arms, but manage somehow. I make my way through the living area and to my bedroom and lay him in my bed before sliding his coat and shoes off, and tucking him in.

I make some chili while he sleeps, and when he wakes he's a bit more lucid and more than ready to eat. We snuggle up on the sofa and watch a documentary on Amazon Prime titled *Secrets of the Octopus*.

"You feeling okay?" I ask him, breathing in his scent and feeling his curls tickling my chin. He nods.

"Fine, just a little sleepy still."

He makes it through the documentary before he's nodding off on my shoulder, and I help him to bed.

Lying next to him that night I card my fingers through his curls as he snores softly, his nasal strip in place, kitty cat mask over his eyes, and his glasses on the nightstand next to him.

I can't help thinking how much better my life has been since I met him, since he moved in with me. How lucky I have been to have known him, that he's willing to share any part of his life with me, that he wants to be with me in any capacity at all, because I know he doesn't have to be.

I can't help thinking about what it does to me to have him sharing my bed, waking up next to him every morning, seeing that smile. I can't help thinking that I don't want to ever wake up to anything but his small body curled up against mine and his curls tickling my face. I don't ever want to wake up and not see those glasses on the nightstand or him wrapped in one of my T-shirts.

I don't know how long it's supposed to take to fall in love with someone, because I've never been in love before. But I think, maybe when you find the right person, it takes hardly any time at all.

THIRTEEN

RORY

I wake to soft kisses on my neck and a gentle hand stroking my belly. I hum softly and nestle back against Parker, soaking up his body heat and the warmth it provides. His fingers skate up my abdomen and I moan, shoving my ass against his crotch when he starts playing with my nipples. I'm hard in an instant and I can feel his rock hard cock pressed against my ass as I move against him.

"Jesus, little rabbit," he murmurs, his voice husky as he meets my thrusts and rubs his thumb slowly over one nipple, making me shiver.

Today is the Wednesday before Thanksgiving. We'll be packing and heading out on the road to make our way to my parents' house, but I need an orgasm first or I'll be hard the entire trip. Parker knows just how to turn me on, and playing with my nipples is a sure fire way to get me horny.

But I didn't brush my teeth last night before bed and I'm sure my breath is terrible. "God, I want you," I tell him, "but can I brush my teeth first? And pee?"

He chuckles. "Why don't we both do that, and then we can shower together?"

I nod and scramble out of bed. He chuckles again at how quickly I'm moving. I hurry down the hall and brush my teeth and pee before making my way back to his room and the master bath. He's got the shower turned on already and is stripping out of his pajama pants and boxers. Seeing him tenting his boxers so prominently is ridiculously hot. They've already got a wet spot on them and I'm still so amazed that he gets this turned on because of me.

My mouth waters when his boxers fall to the floor and his cock is standing tall between his muscular thighs and oozing precum. I want it in my mouth so bad I let out a whimper.

He grins and then kisses me, his huge dick poking me in the belly and leaving precum on my shirt.

I rush to undress when he starts to stroke himself in front of me. Oh fuck. I'm removing my clothes so fast I trip over my pants and stumble, but catch myself on the sink and flush. Parker grins wider.

"Don't hurt yourself," he says. "I'm not going anywhere."

When I'm finally naked he takes my hand and pulls me into the shower with him. I'm climbing him in an instant and my body is electrified at the sensations of his wet, warm skin against mine. He grips my thighs and picks me up, and I wrap my legs around his waist as the water rains down over us and we make out, sucking on each other's tongues and moaning loudly.

"Oh fuck, little rabbit," he murmurs, pulling away. "You sound so hot when you make those noises." He presses me against the wall and I gasp as my back hits the cold tiles. Then he's kissing me again, his cock pressed against my ass crack, and mine hard against his stomach. God, his cock feels amazing just nestled between my cheeks and sliding along my taint.

"Oh, god," I gasp, bucking my hips, my dick rubbing up against his abs, providing the perfect amount of friction, and my asshole fluttering repeatedly at the sensation of his cock sliding over it.

"Shit, I love when you get so darn needy," he rasps, then sucks on my neck, making me moan even louder and rut against him even more. "Oh, god, your ass feels amazing, baby."

Oh fuck. He's never called me that before, and I shiver, my dick oozing precum at his words. "I…I…oh, fuck. I want…" I want everything. I want to keep doing what we're doing, but I want to blow him, too, and I want to frot, and I also have this sudden aching desire to be inside him. Like my dick just fucking needs it. Needs him. I've never felt that before but it sends a surge of pleasure racing through me and my cock spasms as I cry out, my release barreling through me like a fucking Mack truck, and I spray all over his abdomen. Seconds later I feel him tensing, and then a familiar warmth against my ass crack and sliding down my thighs.

He presses kisses to my neck and jaw and then lets me down. We're both breathing heavily as he takes me in his arms and presses another kiss to my head. "Sorry you didn't get to blow me," he says, and I grin, looking up at him.

"It was worth it." He glances down to see that I'm still hard. I flush and he grins.

"I was thinking," he says, his eyes darting to the floor and then back to me as his cheeks flush. "You can say no, of course, but how would you feel about fucking? I know you aren't a fan of bottoming because it hasn't been good in the past, but you know you don't have to be the bottom, right? I mean, I could, and I'd like to, actually, if you're okay with it."

My dick twitches. It's like he's read my mind. Up until now it honestly hadn't occurred to me that I didn't have to bottom because I always have in the past, and because I'm so much smaller than Parker I just assumed he wouldn't want to. The more I think about the idea of topping him, though, the harder I get. But even though I'm excited, I hesitate. "I'm not very big," I tell him. "It might not be very good."

He grins and reaches down, starting to stroke me. I hiss

and then moan. "You know how I feel about your dick," he tells me. "I'm crazy about it. And I want it inside me. If you want that, too."

I nod and he beams. We wash off and then dry off, before we make our way to the bed. Parker is hard again and my dick is throbbing now at the idea of being inside him, having that big, beautiful ass surrounding me and making him come on my cock.

"I think it might work best if we try it lying on our sides," he tells me and I nod. "At least the first time."

"Have you ever bottomed before?" I ask.

He shakes his head. "No, but I'm ready to try it with you. I've used toys on myself a couple of times, but that's it."

I flush and my heart skips a beat. "Okay," I say, my voice soft. He grabs lube and a condom out of his nightstand and tosses them on the bed, then lies down facing away from me and I climb on behind him. "Do you want me to prep you, or do you want to do it?"

He looks over his shoulder at me. I'm shaking slightly, a mixture of anxiety and excitement at the idea of fucking him.

"I'm fine either way," he says. "Are you nervous?"

I nod. "A little, but I want to do this with you, too. I just don't want to hurt you. I've never topped before either. The only person I've ever prepped is myself."

He rolls onto his back so he's staring up at me, and squeezes my arm. "I trust you. And I'd like you to do it. But I don't want you to do anything you don't want to do."

I let out a breath. "Okay, I'll do it. But tell me if I'm hurting you."

He nods and slides his top leg out in front of him, jutting his ass out to grant me access to his hole. I squirt some lube on my finger, and kneel next to him. I groan, watching as he strokes himself. God, that's hot. His dick is so fucking beautiful. Long and thick, and oozing precum once again. I whimper, desperate to have it in my mouth.

He looks over at me and a smile crosses his face that I don't think I've ever seen before. There's mischief there and a tinge of wickedness.

"You're being mean," I pout. He chuckles and I point a finger at him. "I'm gonna fuck you and after I come you're gonna roll over and let me suck your cock."

His eyes widen and then a huge smile breaks out across his face. "Yes, sir," he says, then wiggles his ass at me. I can't help laughing, but I slap his ass at the same time and he yelps slightly. I slide my fingers between his cheeks and circle his hole slowly. He closes his eyes and moans instantly, and it spurs me on.

He whimpers as I slide my finger along his taint. His cock twitches and he pushes his ass back. "That's really good," he whines. "God, it never feels that good when I do it. Don't stop, little rabbit."

God, I'm on cloud nine knowing how good I'm making him feel with just my fingers. This is a fucking rush. My cock jerks and precum leaks out in droves. I slide my finger up his crack and press it against his hole and he spasms, his hole fluttering like crazy against my finger. Holy hell.

"Shit," I breathe. I move my finger away to gather more lube on it and he whimpers, jutting his ass out more.

"Rory." He says my name like he's desperate for me, and shit that does something for me. My cock jerks, and I have to squeeze it to keep from coming.

"Almost there." I slide my finger along his hole again, then press inside gently, and his whole body shudders. Fuck, he responds so well that I can't help wondering if maybe he was right about bottoming being amazing if you do it right.

I stretch him, slowly, moving my finger in and out. He jolts when I press against a soft rubbery spot. "Oh, fuck. Yeah, that's it. More, little rabbit. Please?" He strokes himself and I add a second finger, scissoring them. Then I'm adding more lube to my fingers again and a third slides in this time.

"Fuck," he whines. "I'm ready. I need you, freckles. Fuck me."

Oh, boy. I want this, and my cock really wants this. It's so hard it fucking hurts, but I'm still nervous about my ability to make it good for him. I slide my fingers out and tear open the condom wrapper, sliding it over my dick and then slicking it up with more lube. Then I lie on my side and position my dick at his entrance. *Fuck, here goes nothing.*

I push and the tip of my cock slowly enters him. Oh my god, I fucking shake at the sensation of his ass, hot and tight around me. Holy hell, I've never felt anything like this before. I breathe in and out as I reach around and rest my hand on his abdomen, as he strokes himself slowly. "Oh fuck," I gasp as I position my top leg over his and slide further inside him. "Fuck, this feels amazing. I don't think I'm gonna last long."

"That's okay," Parker breathes. I drink in his toasted marshmallow and vanilla scent and press kisses to his back.

"Are you okay?" I ask.

He nods. "Yeah. Fuck, it feels good, little rabbit. Love your dick, just like I knew I would. So fucking cute and so amazing inside me. Get it in there all the way and fuck me."

I push again and slide all the way in, encased in his tight heat, my breath ragged. I press more kisses to his naked skin and rub circles on his belly. He's still stroking himself slowly.

"Fuck, yeah," he grunts. "Now move. Let me feel you, baby."

I slide out a little bit and then back in and he moans, his hole spasming around me. Oh fuck. I slide all the way out and then back in, and sweat breaks out across his back and neck. The feel of his hard, muscular body against mine is incredible as I move inside him. Every inch of my body is electrified and I am so damn hard.

"Fuck, little rabbit, don't stop. Want you to come inside me. You feel so fucking good. Your little cock is perfect for me."

My cock jerks at his words and I feel my balls drawing up. I thrust harder, gripping him and holding him to me. He stops stroking himself and laces his fingers with mine on his belly. "That's it," he says, "Yes, yes, oh fuck, Rory, yes. Come inside me."

"Oh, fuck!" I cry out and my cock sprays my release inside the condom as my body shakes. Holy hell. I wait about two seconds before I'm sliding out of him slowly.

His eyes are hooded and sweat is beaded on his forehead. His cock is leaking profusely, and I want it in my mouth right fucking now. "Roll over."

He does, and spreads his legs instantly. Damn, that's hot. I position myself between his thighs. Why does everything we're doing together feel so right? "You gonna suck me, little rabbit?" he asks, holding his dick out for me. I lean forward and let my lips slide against the head of his dick, his precum glossing them before I lick it off and then kiss the head of his beautiful cock. Then I lower my head, sliding my tongue along his balls and up his shaft slowly, before taking him in my mouth.

I hum as his taste explodes on my tongue and he groans. I open my eyes for an instant to see his head fallen back against the pillow and his eyes closed, his sexy af Adam's apple bobbing. Then I close my eyes again and take him deeper.

"Oh shit," he cries out, his hips bucking and his cock sliding even further down my throat. My eyes water and saliva and snot slide down my face but I don't ask him to stop. I love it. All of it. The weight of him in my mouth, his taste, the way his cock jerks inside me, the glide of it. It's euphoric. My own cock is half hard again and I reach down and stroke myself as I bob up and down on his dick and let him face fuck me. He grips my hair tight enough to hurt, but I don't let up.

"Oh, fuck, Rory," he moans. "Fuck, so good. I'm gonna come." He thrusts two more times and his grip on my hair tightens as his body spasms and his cock pulses in my mouth.

I swallow everything before he releases my hair and I slide off of him with a pop, my saliva dripping onto his belly and dick.

"Fuck, did I hurt you?" he says, and I shake my head. He grabs a tissue and uses it to wipe my face. Then he's pulling me to him and we kiss languidly, me sprawled on top of him.

"That was amazing," I say, resting my head on his chest as his arms come around me.

"Fuck, yeah, it was," he agrees. "Told you I'd love your dick."

I grin, and he kisses the top of my head before playing with my curls.

A moment passes, my heart beating faster again as I trace his pec with my finger. "Are we exclusive?" I blurt. My face is warm and I think I might puke, but at least I fucking said it. I close my eyes and breathe in and out slowly. His fingers stop and my eyes open. I raise my head and meet his gaze. His hazel eyes are warm and soft.

"I don't want anyone else," he says. "I haven't wanted anyone else."

I swallow. "Me either." His grin is bright and he kisses me again.

PARKER

We're packed and on the road a couple of hours later. We're taking my car because Rory's is too small for me to manage such a long drive. I have the address for his parents' house plugged into the GPS on my phone, and Ed Sheeran is playing as we make our way through the winding roads, surrounded by snow capped mountains and greenery, with a light dusting of snow. We even see a beaver dam and some elk on our drive.

We stop about half way through and switch drivers. We talk about our families for a good portion of the drive and I love how his face lights up when he mentions his parents and sisters. I can tell he's eager to see them, and it makes me happy. His dad's name is Frank and he is an engineer, and his mom's name is Delilah and she is a music teacher, so she's home with his sisters while they are on break. I find out that they make turkey cookies every year, which I can't imagine taste good, until he clarifies that they are cookies shaped like turkeys, not turkey flavored cookies. He tells me they put their tree up the day after Thanksgiving every year so I'll be around for the festivities, and that they have a fire pit in their backyard where they roast smores on Thanksgiving evening after a late lunch.

When we arrive at his house it's evening. I take it in. Two stories, a three car garage, and a well landscaped but small front yard. It looks homey and well taken care of.

"Ready?" Rory says, and I nod. As soon as we step out of the car, the front door opens and a stout woman with dark hair comes racing down the steps and throws her arms around Rory. She hugs him so tight he lets out a pained squeak.

"For Christ's sake, Delilah," a voice that sounds very similar to Rory's says. I look up to see a man a few inches taller than Rory but still several inches shorter than me standing on the front porch in jeans and a flannel shirt, with a baseball cap on. "Let the boy breathe."

"Oh, hush, you," Rory's mom says, releasing Rory and waving off her husband. She grips Rory's cheeks in her hands. "My baby is home at last."

A second later, the front door opens again and two young girls squeal as they zip past their father and down the stairs, their brown hair a blur and wide smiles on their faces as they shout, "Rory!!!" Rory opens his arms and beams as they jump into them. His mom turns to me at the same time and I hold out my hand, but she wraps her arms around me instead, and I bend over to hug her. She smells like spiced apples and cinnamon.

"It's so good to meet you, Parker," she says. "I'm so glad you could join us." She grips my cheeks now. "So tall," she says, "and so handsome." I flush, and Rory groans as his sisters giggle.

"Thank you for inviting me. I really appreciate it, and so do my parents."

"Oh, it's no trouble at all," she assures me. "You're welcome any time."

"Hi, I'm Ava," one of his sisters says, stepping up to me and holding out her hand. I grin and shake it.

"Nice to meet you," I say.

"Chocolate or vanilla?"

"Um…what?" I ask.

"For when we make cupcakes for the tea party. Chocolate or vanilla?"

I grin. "Chocolate."

She beams. I look past her to her sister who is snug against Rory's side. "Hi," I say with a wave. "I'm Parker, Rory's roommate. You must be Addison. I like your dress."

She beams at me and I see Rory smiling widely, too. "Is Moana your favorite princess?" She nods. "She's pretty cool."

"All right, let's get your things and get inside," Delilah says, waving for Mr. C to come help with the luggage.

Ava takes my hand before I can help carry anything, and pulls me towards the house. I look back at Rory and he shrugs, grinning.

"Okay," Delilah says once we're all inside. "Supper's about ready so why don't you boys take your things up to Rory's room and then we'll eat. You don't mind sharing a room, do you?" she asks me. "We don't have a guest room but it's got an air mattress on the floor you can use."

"That's perfect," I say. I don't want to tell her I'll probably be climbing into bed with Rory, because I'm not sure what he's told them about us, and if she got out an air mattress then I'm guessing they don't know we're sleeping together.

There's a large living area off to the left with a comfortable looking sectional and a wide screen tv above a fireplace. Off to the right is a dining area and windows leading to a fenced in backyard, and the kitchen is just a few feet from the dining area with an island and modern appliances. Stairs off to the left and behind the living room lead up to the second floor and there's a small guest bath as well.

I grab my suitcase and Rory takes his, as we head up the stairs. I follow him and he leads me down the carpeted hallway, past an office, another bathroom, and a room with two single beds decorated in Hello Kitty, before stopping at the door at the end of the hall. The door is part way open already, and he shoves it with his shoulder as he enters. It's not a huge room, but it's decent sized. Big enough for his bed, which is also twin sized, and decorated in a black and gray comforter. There's a double inflatable mattress on the floor next to the bed, along with a dresser, closet and a desk.

I stop just inside the room and take it in. There's framed art work as well as several canvases decorating the walls. Beautiful watercolors and pen and ink sketches of flowers, animals, the mountains.

"Holy cinnamon rolls, freckles, you did all these?" I walk further into the room to get a closer look, admiring them.

"Yeah," Rory says, his cheeks pinkening as he shoves his hands in the pockets of his gray skinny jeans. He's paired them with a red dress shirt today and a polka dot bow tie with white suspenders. He looks scrumptious as always.

"They're amazing."

I look around at the rest of his room. Black curtains hang above his window that looks out over the back yard and there's a picture of his family sitting on his desk along with different art supplies.

"Your parents don't know about us, do they?" I ask, and his face pales. He shakes his head.

"Are you mad?"

"No," I tell him, taking his hand and squeezing it. "Honestly, my family doesn't know either. I didn't really know what to tell them."

"Yeah, I guess I didn't either, and I hadn't even told them about Zach and I breaking up until last week."

"We don't have to tell anyone anything until you're ready," I say, and he smiles at me. I want him to want to tell people, sure, because I am ready to tell people. Rory is amazing and I want my family and friends to know I'm with him, especially after our conversation this morning. But with everything that he's been through lately, I don't want to push him either, and he might be freaked out if I told him I'm pretty sure I'm falling for him.

"Thank you." He stands on his tiptoes and kisses my cheek. I hear a dog barking outside and look at him. "Oh, that's Oreo."

"Boys, dinner!" Delilah shouts up the stairs.

"You have a dog?" I ask.

"Yeah, she's super sweet. Come on. I'll introduce you."

We make our way downstairs and to the dining room and I spot Oreo right away. She's a black lab and her tail waves frantically, her feet clapping against the hardwood floor. There's a cool breeze and she smells like grass and dirt, telling me she just got let inside. She's whimpering excitedly when Rory approaches her, me behind him. He kneels and scratches behind her ears. She licks his face, making him scrunch his face up, and I get down on the floor next to him.

She steps right up to me and smells my face, then offers me a lick as well. "Oreo, no," Delilah scolds as she carries a dish to the table and sets it down. It smells amazing. Frank is filling the glasses with water and the girls are sitting at the table, watching the whole thing and giggling.

"It's okay Mrs. C, I don't mind," I tell her as Rory and I stand and I pet Oreo's head as she pants, her tail still going a mile a minute.

"Oh, none of that Mrs. C stuff. Just call me Delilah, sweetheart."

"Same goes for me," Frank says, patting me on the shoulder before he takes a seat at the table.

"Come on, now, sit down before the food gets cold," Delilah says. I take a seat next to Rory across from the twins and Delilah takes one end of the table while Frank takes the other.

They ask me about my major and how school is going while we eat. Delilah is delighted when I tell them I want to be a teacher or a coach, or both. Frank asks if I play any sports, and I shake my head.

"I played football in high school, for fun, but I'm not super competitive and I realized I liked the coaching side of things more and just working with kids."

I tell them about my family and our different traditions when they ask. How we all used to cram into the same room on Christmas Eve when we were kids and we'd stay up all night playing board games and video games, too excited to fall asleep. How Mom insisted on having a real tree even though she was allergic. How the angel tree topper we have has been missing a wing for ten years because my brothers were fighting over who got to put it on the tree and broke it, and Mom couldn't bring herself to get rid of it because after she scolded them it was a fond memory. How we go caroling every year even though none of us can sing except Hope, but we enjoy the time as a family.

I offer to help clean up dinner when we're finished eating but Delilah waves me away and tells me Frank will help and I'm a guest. I should make myself comfortable. Rory and I end up playing a game of Candy Land with Addison and Ava and then Slap Jack, which Addison is wicked good at, before we call it a night. Tomorrow is Thanksgiving and I'm determined to help some in the kitchen. I can't come eat all their good food and not help out.

I slide under the blankets of my air mattress that night as Rory lies in his bed next to me. The lights are off and the moon casts a glow over his freckled face as he looks at me.

"I'm hoping this doesn't sound too selfish," he says, "and I'm not exactly glad you couldn't go home for break, but I'm really glad you're here."

I chuckle. "Me, too."

"Goodnight," he says.

"Night, freckles."

FOURTEEN

RORY

I wake to a wet tongue on my face, and groan as I shove Oreo away, or try to, anyway. It doesn't work and she's climbing all over me, making the mattress sink in under her weight. It's only when I sit up that I realize I'm on the blow up mattress snuggled against Parker. I don't even remember getting out of my bed last night, but apparently I did. Parker has an arm around me and Oreo is now climbing over me and licking his face, ignoring my attempts to get her off the makeshift bed.

"Bad dog," I tell her in a harsh whisper as Parker jolts. "Off."

I scramble up when I realize that the door is open and my sisters' voices are echoing down the hall. The mattress wobbles underneath me, and I almost topple over on my way to close the door. Oreo is still mauling Parker, demanding attention, when I turn around.

"Fuck." I rest my head against the door and let out a breath. I would have been mortified if Addison and Ava had seen us in bed together, Parker shirtless and me cuddled up against him. I'm still trying to figure out how the door got opened, because I swear it was closed last night when we went to bed. He's sitting up now, scratching Oreo's belly as she lies on her back pressed up against him, her tongue lolling out and feet in the air.

"I'm gonna go shower," I tell him.

When I get back to the room, Oreo is gone and Parker is pulling things out of his suitcase. I close the door and move over to him. "You sleep okay?" I ask.

"Never better." His eyes are bright and he's smiling widely. I can't help it. I press a kiss to his lips.

"You okay with me sharing the bed with you?"

"Of course. I was kinda hoping you would. Maybe we should lock the door tonight, though, if you're worried about your family."

I wince. "Sorry. It's not you, at all. I promise. I just–"

He places a finger against my lips. "You don't have to explain yourself, freckles. I understand. I'm not offended. Nothing until you're ready. Remember?"

I nod. God, if he only knew how crazy I am about him. How I want to tell everyone that we're together and that he makes me happier than I've ever been before. But I feel like maybe it's too soon? Maybe I need to let them adjust to the idea of me not being with Zach before I tell them I'm head over heels for Parker. Or maybe there's a little part of me that's still scared, that somehow if I say something it will all come crashing down.

He kisses me again and then makes his way across the hall to the bathroom. I head downstairs and inhale the scent of Mom's cinnamon rolls. My mouth waters and I grab one, gobbling it down as Ava and Addison come running down the hall in fairy outfits and holding wands.

They race over and hug me as soon as they see me. "Will you and Parker play with us?" Ava asks, blinking those big brown eyes at me.

"Breakfast first, and then we can. Where are Mom and Dad?"

"Daddy is in the basement and Mommy is walking Oreo. She said only one cinnamon roll, and lunch is at two."

I look at the clock on the stove. It's ten o'clock now.

Parker enters the room just then, in a pair of snug fitting jeans that show off his very fine ass, and a black T-shirt that clings to his body like a second skin. I bite my lip to keep from moaning at the sight of him, his hair damp and those gorgeous biceps bulging without him even trying.

"Hello, my fair fairies," he says, bowing to Ava and Addison, making them giggle in delight.

"Rory said you'll play with us after you eat," Ava announces. I flush and look at Parker.

"Only if Parker is okay with it."

He grins. "Of course. But only if I get to be a fairy, too." He winks at them and they giggle again.

While they are off finding dress up clothes for us to wear, we eat our breakfast. The girls return with a pair of dress up wings for Parker along with a tulle skirt that I have no idea how it will fit him. Addison hands me a crown and a feather boa.

"You get to be the princess," she says, grinning at me.

"Is this your new crown?" I ask, admiring the silver headpiece adorned with different colored jewels. She beams and nods.

Parker stands and slides into the wings and tutu, and I can't help snorting and chuckling at the sight. It's a good thing the tulle skirt has an elastic waistband. He's so big everything looks tiny on him, but he's so confident, it's kind of sexy at the same time, and I love how he's interacting with my sisters.

We're in the living room when Dad comes up the stairs and spots us. Parker is prancing around with Ava and Addison and I'm sitting on my regal throne, aka, the rocking chair, as they entertain me. I do think I have the best role in this game of make believe. Dad tries to hide his amusement as he watches us but he isn't very successful. He has his hand over his mouth but his eyes are twinkling.

When Mom returns from walking Oreo, Oreo bounds into the living room, wanting to join the fun.

Pretty soon the house smells like apples, nutmeg, and freshly baked bread, as Mom gets to work in the kitchen.

Parker pauses the game to ask if we should help in the kitchen. "You can try," I tell him, "but she won't let you."

He does, and she doesn't. I hear, "Oh, no, dear, thank you. I've got everything handled. You go have fun."

He shrugs and I mouth *told you* when he returns.

We do help set the table later though, and that seems to make Parker happy. The meal is amazing as always, and I groan as Mom and Dad share stories of when I was little.

"He was so cute," Mom coos, looking at me. "He's been wearing bow ties since he was six years old, you know. All the other boys were in jeans and T-shirts, but not Rory. He's always loved to dress up."

"Do you have pictures?" Parker asks, and I bury my face in my hands when Mom nods, a huge smile on her face.

"We'll show you after dinner."

Parker grins at me and I glare, but it's not real. I can't be mad at him or my parents.

"You should have seen him when the girls came along," Dad says. "He was such a good big brother. Scared shitless at first, but once they were here you couldn't get him to stop holding them and wanting to help."

I flush, and Ava and Addison beam at me. I stick my tongue out at them and they giggle.

After lunch, Dad goes away and comes back with a photo album. He sits on the sofa and Parker joins him. They flip through it as I help Mom with the dishes, and the twins race upstairs to their room.

"He's a really sweet boy," Mom tells me, and I hear Parker and Dad laughing in the next room.

"He is," I agree.

There's a short pause before she says, "You know you don't have to tell me what happened with you and Zach, but I'm here to listen if you want to."

I don't know what happens. Maybe it's the fact that she's my mom, or maybe I've been holding it all in more than I realized, or maybe it's the thanksgiving turkey messing with my head, but I start sobbing right then and there, and she takes me into her arms, holding me close as Dad and Parker continue to laugh in the next room, and I hear shrieks and squeals from upstairs. I flinch and Mom rubs my back, shushing me softly.

"I'll get them set up with a movie in a bit," she says, knowing how I need the quiet, no matter how much I love my sisters. "It's okay. You're okay."

I sniffle and choke out. "He cheated on me."

"Oh, honey," she says, hugging me harder and making me cry more. "I'm so sorry. That must have felt terrible."

I word vomit then, telling her about how I found him, all the texts he sent me afterwards, the things he said, how he made me feel like I wasn't good enough and how somehow it was my fault, and how I realized what a complete asshole he was. I tell her how I've been struggling with believing I'm good enough and that anyone would ever want me because of how he made me feel. She listens and strokes my hair, and kisses my head.

"My beautiful boy," she murmurs. "You are such a kind soul and you deserve someone who appreciates you. I'm really glad you're not with him anymore. But I am sorry he hurt you."

She hands me a tissue and I use it to wipe my nose. "Yeah, me, too." She hugs me again and I melt into her. "Thank you."

Dad and Parker enter the kitchen then and Dad stops when he sees us hugging. Parker looks a little concerned, too.

"Everything okay?" Dad asks.

I nod and Mom smiles at him in a way that says, *I'll tell you later.*

Dad shows us a picture in the album of me at the age of six riding my big wheel bike, a huge smile on my face, my two front teeth missing.

"You were the cutest little kid, freckles," Parker says, ruffling my hair and making me blush. Mom and Dad exchange glances at the nickname and my cheeks heat.

There's another shriek from upstairs and I flinch again.

"I'll take care of it," Mom says. She kisses my cheek and heads up the stairs.

I tell Mom and Dad that Parker and I are going to take a nap in my room. Dad reminds us that s'mores start at six and I nod, then grab Parker's hand and pull him up to the stairs.

We lie on the blow up mattress and make out for a while before we doze off, this time with the door locked.

PARKER

Rory and I find several moments over the next few days to "take a nap" so we can have an excuse to go into his room and make out. And we may run errands together so we can find secluded spots to fuck. I'm loving being with him and his family, but I can't go days at a time without touching him or I'll go nutsy cuckoo. I know it's fast, but I'm falling for him harder and harder, and seeing him with his family, in this new environment, is just solidifying those feelings.

The day after Thanksgiving we set up the tree just like he said we would, and even though I didn't feel like I should be joining in on a family moment and was content to sit and watch, sipping hot chocolate, both Frank and Delilah insisted that I am "part of the family" and practically shoved ornaments into my hands. Ava and Addison were all too eager to have me help, and I even picked them up so they could reach the tallest branches on the tree, which had them squealing with glee.

Rory looked at me in a way I'd never seen before, stars shining in his eyes and his cheeks rosy. I took him up to his room afterwards and we rutted against each other, our lips locked, until we both came in our pants. We cleaned up and then I held him as we napped. I can't help smiling at the fact that even though the air mattress can't be as comfortable as his bed, he's still sleeping on it with me because he wants to be close.

We made the turkey cookies from Oreos, candy corn and Reese's cups, and then Rory coaxed me into baking my cupcakes for the tea party we had with the twins. I think maybe he just wanted an excuse to leave the house and pick up ingredients so we could have another chance to make out, but I was completely on board with that.

Right now he's straddling me in the backseat of my car and whimpering as I grip us and stroke us together. The dry humping we've done in his room is great, but it's risky and he always struggles to be quiet, which I know makes him nervous, and then he doesn't enjoy himself as much. It's also fast, and while I can't complain about any moment I have with Rory, I like not feeling rushed, so finding moments to leave the house is essential, and I am drinking up his sexy as fuck noises now. I can't get enough of them.

"Oh fuck," he mewls as he watches me, bucking his hips, my hand tight around us as I stroke us in tandem. We're both mostly dressed, with just our pants down slightly and our dicks out, and I really wish we could be naked, but again, risky. And I don't want to make Rory nervous.

His bright pink thong is under his balls and the thin straps are stretched across his hips. His hair is mussed, his glasses fogged up, and his lips swollen and puffy from our kissing. It's the fucking hottest thing I've ever seen. I grip his plump little ass with my other hand and squeeze and he moans, gripping my shoulders harder and thrusting into my hand faster, his dick sliding along mine and making me shiver.

"You feel amazing, freckles," I tell him, out of breath.

"Love your cock so much." His dick jerks in my grip and precum oozes out. I stroke us faster and harder, the glide slick with lube and precum.

"Oh, god," he moans, his head thrown back and his gorgeous neck on display. I growl and lick it, then bite down as he shakes. "Oh, fuck. Yes. God, yes, Parker. Don't stop. I'm so close. So good."

"Fuck, little rabbit, you drive me insane. So fucking pretty." I nibble on his collarbone as I stroke us and feel my own climax building.

"Again," he begs and I lick his neck before biting down again. His orgasm erupts, cum shooting out and coating my hands and dick. I release him as he trembles and then I stroke myself while he watches.

I'm coming seconds later, spraying across his dick and balls as I howl his name. We rest for a moment before cleaning up with some wipes and tucking ourselves away again. Then we sit in the car and snuggle for a little bit.

"I know we haven't done any more anal sex yet, since we've been here," he says, "but I would be up for more when we get back home."

He looks up at me and I straighten out his glasses, making him grin. I kiss the top of his head. "Me, too."

On Sunday we say goodbye to Rory's family in the driveway, and the twins and Delilah have tears in their eyes. Oreo is there, too, tail wagging like crazy and tongue out as she weaves in between all of us, demanding attention. I crouch and scratch behind her ears. She licks my face.

"Thanks for sharing your family with me," I tell her. She licks me again and I laugh as I push myself back to my feet.

"Don't be a stranger around here," Frank says as he shakes my hand. "We loved having you and you're welcome any time."

"Don't go!" Ava cries as she hugs Rory tightly.

"I'll be back in three weeks," he promises.

"With Parker?" Addison asks in her soft voice. My chest squeezes at the disappointment on her face when Rory shakes his head.

"I'll be with my family for Christmas," I tell her. Ava crosses her arms and pouts and I think Addison might cry for real this time. She throws her arms around me, her head against my stomach as she squeezes me. "I had a lot of fun with you guys, though. Maybe I can come back over another break. And if it's okay with your parents I can say hi to you when Rory talks to you on the phone."

Addison looks up at me with those big brown eyes. Then back at Delilah.

"Mommy, can we talk to Parker on the phone?"

"I think that would be fine, dear," she says, smiling and gesturing for her daughter to step back. "Now, let's let them go. They have to get back."

Addison gives me one more squeeze and then steps away. They're waving as we get into the car and pull out of the driveway, and they keep waving until we're out of sight.

I take Rory's hand as he wipes a tear from his cheek. "You've got an amazing family," I tell him.

"I do," he agrees.

FIFTEEN

PARKER

We're both incredibly busy over the next few weeks, finishing up papers and projects, and studying for final exams. Rory is spending a good chunk of his time in the art studio, working on his final project for the semester in one of his Illustration courses, and we haven't seen much of each other.

We've only had sex a handful of times since we returned from Thanksgiving break, and I'm missing him like crazy. Not just his cute little dick inside me making me blow my load, which we've done a few more times now, but everything about him. His smile, his laugh, his shyness outside the bedroom and his confidence in it. His humor, his tenderness, those adorable freckles, the way he scrunches up his nose. The way he smells and the feel of him in my arms. The way his curls tickle my chin when we're snuggling in bed or on the couch. And the thought of being away from him for two more weeks over Christmas break is making me so sad I'm baking up a storm in whatever spare time I have.

Rory has asked me if I'm okay, which is a fair question when he comes home and sees two dozen cupcakes and just as many cookies decorating the kitchen counters, along with banana bread and brownies. I tell him I'm just stressed about final exams because admitting how much I miss him and don't want to be away from him over break might scare him if he's not feeling the same.

He coaxes me into the bedroom after dinner two nights before break and my dick is hard in an instant when he starts to strip. His red suspenders fall off his shoulders and he shimmies out of his pants, then removes his bowtie and unbuttons his shirt, letting them fall to the floor. My eyes widen. The panties I was expecting, but the rest of it is enough to make me almost come on the spot. He's standing in front of me in a lacy red thong, his cock hard and his face flushed. There's a wet spot forming on his panties already. But the thing that's new is the lacy red bra he's got on, and the sexy as hell red thigh high tights that have lace along the top. I'm actually speechless, but my dick is so fucking hard it hurts as he sashays towards me where I'm sitting on the edge of the bed.

"I've missed you," he says, and just the way he's looking at me has my cock throbbing in my jeans. "And I thought maybe I could give you an early Christmas present. Help you relax a little and give the oven a break."

I chuckle and flush, but he's smiling and presses a kiss to my lips that quickly becomes more heated as he climbs onto my lap and straddles me. I moan as he tilts my head back and slides his tongue down my throat, his fingers gripping my hair as I move my hands to his ass and grip his cheeks. He loves when I play with his ass.

Sure enough, he moans into my mouth and juts his ass out to fill my palms, kissing me harder.

I want to tell him so badly how I feel and it's on the tip of my tongue, but when I pull away from the kiss I say, "I need to get naked."

He nods and climbs off of me so I can strip, and then I'm taking him in my arms and lifting him, his legs wrapped around me. I remove his glasses and set them on the dresser before I carry him to the bed and lower him onto it, his legs still wrapped around me. I love the feel of his silky tights against my skin and I shiver.

"God, you're so fucking pretty," I say, staring into his vivid blue eyes as he gazes up at me, brown curls falling over his forehead. I kiss him again, and when I pull away, I reach for the lube and condoms in the nightstand. His hand grips my wrist and I meet his gaze again.

"I've been thinking," he says. "I think I want to try bottoming, with you."

I stare at him, my heart pounding and my dick leaking precum onto his belly. "Really?" I ask. "You know I'm perfectly happy with what we're doing."

"I know," he tells me. "But I want this. I want to know what it feels like to have you inside me."

"Oh fuck," I whisper. I kiss him languidly and when I pull away say, "I'll be gentle. I'll take care of you, little rabbit. I promise."

"I know you will," he says, and my heart flutters. I kneel, then reach up and grip the waistband of his thong, pulling it over his erection and down, sliding it off his legs and tossing it to the floor. My gaze tracks over him, the silky tights, that cute as fuck dick, the lacy bra, the adorable freckle scattered face, and my breath catches in my throat at how much he means to me. When I speak again, my voice is rough, and barely a whisper.

"I'll stretch you like this," I tell him, "but I think you should ride me, then you can control it more."

He nods, and I slide my hands along his thighs and his belly, drinking him in. I lean forward and press kisses to his abdomen, working my way down to his tummy, right above his dick. I slide my tongue inside his belly button and he sucks in a breath, his stomach sinking in and his body starting to tremble. I press kisses to his hips and thighs, feeling the silky material of his tights against my cheek. Then I move up again and press even more kisses to his cock, and it twitches each and every time as Rory gasps, my name spilling from his lips as his precum slicks up my lips. He tugs on my arms and whines, and when I see the look in his eyes, my breath catches.

He doesn't speak, just tugs once more and I move up and press my lips to his. He whimpers as I slide my tongue in his mouth and his legs come around me again, his fingers tangling in my hair. I slide my hand up his stomach slowly, and then under the band of his bra. He gasps into my mouth as I play with his nipples.

"Parker," he whines, making my cock throb. "Please."

"Fuck, little rabbit. Can't get enough of you."

He whimpers again and bucks his hips up, his arms above his head. Fuck, he's gorgeous like this, and I'm overwhelmed that he is giving me control. I grip his chin and slant my lips over his again, kissing him hard as he rubs up against me, whimpering and moaning into my mouth. When I pull away, his lips are swollen and his eyes are lust blown.

"Need you," he says. "Fuck me."

"Jesus, freckles." I kiss him again before I grab the bottle of lube from the nightstand and slick up my fingers. I don't say anything. He spreads his legs for me and a shiver races down my spine at the sight of his gorgeous little pucker fluttering in anticipation. I can't help it, I lower myself and slide my tongue along his taint, gripping his thighs and spreading his cheeks, the lube on my fingers getting on his tights.

"Oh, sorry," I murmur, and he almost snarls at me as he grips his legs and spreads them wider.

"Get back down there, goddamn it, and do that again."

I grin and return to my task, licking and sucking on his hole as he curses and repeats my name again and again. I slide my tongue inside and he mewls.

"Oh, god. Fuck, fuck, fuck. Stop. Stop." I pull out and wipe the back of my hand across my mouth. He's breathing heavily and his eyes are lidded, his skin flushed. "Fuck, I almost came."

I grin again and kiss his cock. "I wouldn't have minded."

He shakes his head. "I want your cock. I don't want to come until it's buried inside me." He spreads his legs again and I add more lube to my fingers before sliding inside him slowly.

"Oh, god, yes." His head falls back, his neck muscles straining and his mouth parted in bliss. I slide my finger in and out before pegging his prostate and watching him shudder. "Oh, oh, fuck, oh fuck, that's so good. Oh fuck, Parker." I add a second finger and scissor them, and he whimpers.

"You okay?" I ask, and he nods. "You're sexy as fuck, little rabbit. Love your hole."

"It feels good," he rasps, looking at me as I continue to move my fingers inside him, slowly, gently. "I've....ngggg, I've never had it feel this good before." Tears fill his eyes and slide down his cheeks and his chest heaves.

"Oh, baby," I croon, my fingers stilling, my heart a mixture of pain that he never had a good experience bottoming before, and pride that I'm the one giving it to him now.

"I'm sorry," he says, wiping at his cheeks. "That's not very sexy."

"It's okay to cry," I tell him. "Crying during sex isn't uncommon. You've got lots of hormones doing crazy things and you're feeling a lot. I won't ever judge you for crying. You can feel however you need to feel with me."

He nods and gives me a small smile.

"Do we need to stop?"

He shakes his head, so I kiss him gently and then start moving again. A few more tears slip free as I stretch him, but we don't stop.

"You still good?" I ask when my fingers slide out.

"Yes," he says. "I don't want to ride you, though. I want to be under you."

I look into his eyes and nod. "Okay." I slick up my cock and position myself at his entrance. "It will hurt some, but I promise it will feel good, too. If it doesn't, if you don't like it for any reason, we'll stop. Just say the word. I'm trusting you to tell me if you want to stop."

He nods and I rest my hands on either side of him before I push in slowly. I did a good job stretching him and I slide past his tight ring with not much effort. He hisses and lets out a breath, and I lean over, kissing him, and sliding my free hand under his bra again, circling his hard nipple with my thumb. I slide in a little more as he grips my cheeks and kisses me back, whimpering softly into my mouth. I pull away from the kiss and rest my forehead against his, our breaths mingling between us as my thumb and forefinger continue to play with his nipple and he shivers.

"You're really big," he whispers.

I nod. "You feel amazing. I'm gonna come most of the way out and then slide back in."

He nods this time and I slide slowly out, before coating my cock in more lube and pressing back in. He gasps as I slide almost all the way in and my body shudders at how fucking incredible it feels to be inside him. To have his perfect little ass swallowing my cock. "Fuck, freckles, you feel good." I breathe in and out and so does he, and then I'm sliding all the way inside him, buried deep, my cock throbbing and my body shaking with the need to move, to fuck him.

More tears slide down his cheeks now and I press my forehead to his. "Please say those are good tears," I whisper, and he nods as even more tears fall, his body shaking.

"I can't believe you're inside me."

"Fuck, freckles, I'm gonna cry if you keep saying stuff like that."

He chuckles and lets out a breath. "It hurts, but it also feels really fucking amazing. Like a really pleasant burn." He wipes his tears and I kiss his nose.

"If I do my job right it should feel a whole lot better in a couple of seconds," I tell him. "I'm gonna move now. You feel so fucking good, and I don't think I'm gonna last long."

He nods and I slide out before pushing back in. He clings

to me, arms and legs wrapped around me as I gradually increase the speed and severity of my thrusts, his breaths picking up and his cries of pleasure getting louder and louder as I fuck him. Holy shit, I am crying now. I know beyond the shadow of a doubt that I'm in love with my little roomie.

I wrap my arms around him, holding his small body to me, and thrust again and again. His silky tights rub against my sides and his lacy bra brushes against my chest, sending even more shockwaves of pleasure through me as I fuck him.

"Parker," he cries, his grip on me tightening. "Fuck, don't stop. Love your cock." I thrust harder and nail his prostate again and again. "Oh, god. More. Please, Parker, more. I need you."

Shit, I can't control myself when he says things like that. I thrust hard and fast and he's sobbing underneath me as I press kisses to his neck and jaw.

"Come for me, little rabbit," I say. I thrust two more times and he explodes, his back arching as his hole clenches around me, his cock spurting his release between us. I'm so close it only takes two more thrusts before I'm joining him, my cum filling the condom buried inside him.

I don't collapse on him. I'm afraid I might hurt him if I do. Instead I pull out slowly, then keep him in my arms and roll onto my back, bringing him with me so he's lying on top of me now.

He doesn't speak for a while, just cries more, and I run my fingers through his hair as his body shakes.

"You okay, little rabbit?" I ask eventually. He lifts his head and his eyes meet mine. He still doesn't say anything, just kisses me.

"Come to my art show tomorrow night?" he says, and I blink. "Well, not my art show. The school's art show. They're showcasing all the final projects and I really want to show you mine."

"Of course," I tell him, and he kisses me again. He doesn't say anything after that and I slide out from under him to get a washcloth and clean us off. Then I climb back into bed naked and curl up against him as we fall asleep.

Rory has to leave early the following evening to be at the art show before it starts. I know Lucy and Jackson will be there too, and I'm way excited to see what he's done. I know it will be amazeballs.

Tomorrow night is our Christmas/yay we finished finals and didn't die, party at Lucy's place, and then the following morning Rory is dropping me off at the airport and then heading home for Christmas. I know I should be more excited about seeing my family, and I really do want to see them, but I'll hate being away from my little rabbit for two whole weeks.

"Oh, shit," I say, mouth gaping as Rory comes into the living room dressed in a tux. I've never seen him this dressed up before, and he's cute af. I take his hand in mine and press my lips to his fingers. He squirms and bites his lip.

"You look amazing," I tell him.

He flushes and presses up on his tiptoes to kiss me. "See you soon," he says, then grabs his coat and heads out the door.

I shower and dress, then text Jackson and Lucy to let them know I'm on my way. They say they'll meet me outside and we can go in together.

It's a short drive, and I'm there in less than five minutes. It's dark out since it's evening in December, and the pathway up to the front door of the art building is lined with snow, and lit up by street lights. I can see the crowd gathering through the large windows and the glass front doors, and more and more people are arriving every second and making their way inside.

Lucy and Jackson are just inside and I smile when I see them. Lucy hugs me and kisses my cheek. Jackson looks a little off, though, with dark circles under his eyes and his hair not styled to perfection as usual. He doesn't say anything, just stands with his hands in his pockets and his shoulders slumped.

"You okay?" I ask.

He nods, and when his phone buzzes he takes it out of his pocket, looks at it, and then slides it away again without responding to whoever it was, but his cheeks are flushed and he looks even more upset now.

We make our way through the crowded hallway, filled with different pieces of art; drawings, paintings, photographs. They're all amazing, but I know before I see it that I will love Rory's the best.

We spot him, and Lucy and I weave our way through the crowd over to where he's standing next to his piece, Jackson trailing behind us, looking at his phone again. He's clearly bothered by something and doesn't want to tell us what, but this night is about Rory, so I turn my attention to him again, and the gorgeous watercolor he's painted that is displayed on the easel next to him. Underneath it is the title: "Parker."

My eyes widen and I look at him.

"Is that me?" I say, and he bites his lip, nodding. He's painted a picture of me lying in bed on my stomach with the sheet over my bottom half, my bare back on display and the sunlight spilling through the window, casting shadows over my face. It's incredible.

"It's amazing, Rory," Lucy says, and kisses his cheek.

"How did you do that without me noticing?" I ask, still in disbelief.

"I took a picture of you and then worked off of it. Are you mad?"

"What?" I say. "Mad? No, I'm honored. I can't believe you picked me for your final project. It's so good."

He beams and I kiss his cheek. When I turn, Lucy is having a hushed conversation with Jackson a few feet away.

"Is he okay?" Rory asks.

"I don't know," I tell him.

"He's been acting weird lately. Moody, and closed off, and I don't know what's going on. He won't talk to either me or Lucy about what's bugging him." He hesitates for a second before asking, "Is Preston okay?"

"I don't know," I say. "He's seemed okay in class, but I haven't really talked with him outside it in a while. Before break, though, he was acting kind of weird, blowing the guys and I off because he had 'plans'." I put the word in finger quotes. "Why?"

"I heard them arguing at the party we had right before Thanksgiving and I think maybe they're fighting."

My eyes widen. "You think they're together?"

"I don't know. Maybe. Like I said, he won't tell us anything. But remember the Halloween party?"

"Oh, shit. Yeah, they were flirting weren't they?" He nods and then we see Jackson looking in our direction and Lucy whispering something to him. He makes his way over to us and gives Rory a hug.

"I'm sorry I'm being an asshole," he says.

"It's okay," Rory says.

"No, it's not. Things are fucked up right now but you're my best friend and tonight is your night. I'm really proud of you, babe."

"Thank you." Rory gives a small smile, but I can tell he's worried about his friend.

We leave shortly after that, and Rory stays behind as more people come through to view his work and congratulate him. It's late by the time he gets back to the apartment and toes off his dress shoes. He looks exhausted.

I pat my leg and he lies on the couch with his head in my lap while I massage his scalp. He's snoring only minutes later and I carry him to bed.

RORY

The following day we don't have classes. We're finished with finals and we leave tomorrow to go home for Christmas break. I'm beyond excited to see my family again and watch Ava and Addison get their green belts in martial arts, but I've also been pretty melancholy about the fact that I won't see Parker for two weeks. No kisses, no hand holding, no cuddles, no sex.

I've finally had to admit to myself that I'm head over heels for him, but I'm scared it's too soon and I don't want to say anything yet. I don't know what the right timing is for this stuff. I just know he's it for me.

We sleep in and then fuck in the shower. We pack and then fuck again. I feel like I can't get enough of him knowing I'll be dropping him off tomorrow and that he'll be all the way in California. Will he want me to call him? Or will he be too busy having fun with his family to talk to me?

We eat dinner early and then head over to Lucy's around eight. Parker is dressed in an ugly Christmas sweater and jeans and I'm wearing a red shirt with a green bow tie and black suspenders. I also have reindeer antlers on my head and of course, my earplugs.

Her apartment is about a ten minute drive and when we arrive we hear Christmas music playing from the other side of the door as we stand in the hallway. I knock and the door opens a moment later. It's one of Lucy's roommates and she smiles and ushers us inside. We join the rapidly growing crowd of people, chatting, laughing, and drinking. There's several new faces. Jackson is here, as well as some classmates of Lucy's and her roommate's friends. Chris, Blake and Preston are here too. And I can't help noticing how Preston and Jackson are staying on opposite ends of the room from each other, but glancing at the other constantly.

Parker and I head to the kitchen to grab a drink. We chat with Lucy for a minute before she gets whisked away by a girl with red hair and very ample breasts who's dressed in what can only be described as a Santa Claus jumpsuit, and a headband with blinking Christmas lights on it.

Preston stumbles into the kitchen a second later with a drink in his hand. His face is slack and his lips are pressed into a thin line as he puts his cup down and loads up a plate with snacks.

"Hey, you okay?" Parker asks.

"Yeah, sure." Preston's reply is clipped and he shoves a chip in his mouth, crunching down on it hard.

I exchange a look with Parker and he shrugs. "How were finals?" he tries again.

"Great," Preston says. "Amazing. Fucking fantastic."

I hear a laugh from the next room that I know is Jackson, and Preston's body tenses. He eats more. As I get a closer look at him I can see that he is definitely not okay. His eyes look red and bloodshot, like he hasn't been sleeping, and I've never seen him this worked up before. He's clearly pissed, and I have a feeling it's at my best friend. What is going on with those two?

"Listen, I know we haven't talked much lately," Parker says to his friend. "But you know you can talk to me. About anything."

Preston nods. He sounds more tired than upset when he says, "Yeah, thanks. I'm fine, though. Really."

Parker squeezes his shoulder, and we make our way into the living room. There's a makeshift dance area, and on the other side of the room there's a group of people playing some sort of drinking game having to do with Christmas songs.

Parker and I dance for a little bit before we head back into the kitchen for a snack. It's only a few seconds later that I hear Preston's voice coming from the living room, and then a collective gasp. "What the fuck do you think you're doing?"

"Preston, calm down." That's Jackson's voice. Parker and I hurry into the living room to see what's going on. We get there in time to see Preston shove another guy, someone I don't know but who was clearly getting friendly with Jackson.

"Get your fucking hands off him," Preston snarls.

"What the hell?" Jackson says. "Preston, lay off. It's none of your business."

Preston's face is filled with hurt. "Fuck you," he retorts, the entire room staring at the scene in front of us. "I can't do this anymore, Jackson. I'm fucking done. Have a nice life."

He turns to Lucy. "I'm sorry," he says, and he honestly looks like he might cry. Then he's turning and heading for the door.

I look at Parker as the party resumes and then across the room at Jackson, who seems to be torn between staying and leaving as the guy Preston shoved moves back into Jackson's space.

Jackson brushes him off and heads for the door, too. Jesus, what the hell? I look at Lucy and she shakes her head.

We don't stay much longer because I'm exhausted and can't handle the noise. But when we do get back to our apartment I text Jackson to ask if he's okay.

There's no reply.

SIXTEEN

RORY

I'm trying to keep the tears from falling down my cheeks as I drop Parker off at the airport the next morning. The drive wasn't long enough and now we're sitting at the drop off zone with cars zooming around us, and I know I'm gonna get yelled at if I stay too long, so we climb out and I pop the trunk. The cold December air bites at my face as Parker grabs his luggage, and I'm a fucking mess. I'm already missing him so much my chest hurts and my throat is tight when I say, "Have a good break." I can't even meet his eyes because if I do I know I won't be able to keep the tears at bay.

"You, too," he says, his voice soft. "Say hi to your family for me."

I nod, hands in my pockets.

Chilled fingers grip my chin and raise my face. I suck in air but manage not to cry when I'm finally looking at him. His cheeks are already rosy from the cold and his lips are chapped, hazel eyes soft. He's beautiful. And I'm so fucking crazy about him.

He lowers his face to mine and kisses me softly. "See you in a couple weeks."

I nod again as the airport security guard shouts at us to move along. Parker kisses my forehead and then turns and walks away.

I get back in my car and wait for a spot so I can pull out into the traffic again.

As soon as I'm on the interstate, tears are spilling down my cheeks.

It takes me longer than normal to make the drive home because I have to keep pulling over to cry some more, and because I'm distracted I'm not driving the regular speed limit most of the time.

It's late afternoon by the time I pull into the driveway of my childhood home, and it already feels so strange to be here without Parker.

My family is hurrying down the front steps to wrap me in hugs just like always, and Dad grabs my luggage while Mom ushers me inside, Oreo jumping up and down in excitement, her tail wagging frantically.

I make my way up to my room and stare at my phone for a minute, wondering if I should text Parker and tell him I made it safely, ask him if he's home yet? But I just keep staring, because I don't know if he wants to hear from me over break, and I was too scared to ask him before he left.

I slide my phone back in my pocket, looking around my room, and start crying again at how much space there is due to the lack of air mattress. I hate it. I hate being up here by myself. I hate not seeing him interact with my family. I hate that we won't be coming up with excuses to shut ourselves in my room and make out.

I cry for a tiny bit longer and then wipe my tears before heading across the hall to Ava and Addison's room.

"You guys excited for Christmas?" I ask, trying to sound more exuberant than I feel.

They nod and gesture for me to join them. We're playing a game of Would You Rather, when Mom knocks on the door and smiles at us.

"Would you rather have a pet unicorn or a pet dragon?" Ava asks Mom.

"Oh, gosh that's a tough one," Mom says. "Probably a unicorn because dragons are really cool but they might accidently burn something."

"Yeah, but you could fly!" Addison says.

Mom laughs.

"Unicorns can fly, too," Ava says.

"Those are called Alicorns," Addison says, "and you didn't say Alicorn."

"Okay, it's time to get going to the light festival downtown," Mom says, and the girls squeal, jumping to their feet.

I leave to freshen up a bit from the drive and use the bathroom, then head downstairs.

We take Oreo with us and make our way downtown where there's miles of different light up displays to see and enjoy, festive Christmas music playing, an ice skating rink and hot chocolate.

My phone buzzes while we're standing in line for the hot chocolate, and I pull it out to see that Parker has texted me. My heart leaps in my chest and I open the message.

Parker: Hey, little rabbit, thought I'd let you know I made it home safe. I hope you made it home safe, too. I miss you.

Fuck, I have tears filling my eyes and my heart rate spikes even more. He misses me. I let out a breath as I type back.

Me: I made it safely, too. And I miss you too

I wonder if he'll reply or not, but my phone buzzes again a second later.

Parker: Can I Facetime you later tonight? We're heading to Amy's dance recital soon but I need to hear your voice.

Holy shit.

Me: Yes

Parker: smiley face emoji

I'm a little bit more chipper after that and enjoy the evening with my family. After the Christmas festivities we head to a restaurant for dinner, then back home to watch *Home Alone*, an annual tradition for us.

Parker calls while I'm in the kitchen grabbing a snack and I answer it so fast he probably thinks I was staring at the screen.

"Hi," I say, my cheeks flushed and unable to keep the smile from my face. He looks tired but good.

"Hi," he says, smiling back. It looks like he's in his room sitting on the bed.

"How are you?" We both say at the same time, and then laugh. We talk for a little bit about his flight and my drive, then what each of us did that day and what we'll be doing over the rest of the break.

"Hey, dude, I'm on the phone," Parker says, looking away from the screen.

"Ooh, is that the boyfriend?" I hear another male voice say, and feel my cheeks heat. The next thing I know Parker's face is gone and I'm looking at who I assume is one of his brothers. Whether it's Aaron or Archer I have no idea. He's big, like Parker, but not quite as bulky, and his hair is longer. He's not bad on the eyes, but he can't hold a candle to Parker.

"Hey, give it back," Parker says, and I watch as he reaches for the phone and struggles with his brother, who holds the phone away and uses his other arm to hold Parker at bay.

"Hey, boyfriend," Aaron/Archer says.

"Seriously, Archer," Parker says, "give it back or you don't get a single bite of my pumpkin pie tomorrow."

"Ouch, that's harsh," Archer says, but the next thing I know I'm looking at Parker again.

"And go away," Parker adds, shooing his brother.

"Hey, this is my room, too, barf brain."

"It hasn't been your room since you moved in with Aaron. Now get out."

"Fine but Mom and Dad said dinner's ready so you need to get off soon. Bye hottie!" He shouts, and I flush crimson, realizing he's talking to me.

There's the sound of the door closing and then Parker runs his fingers through his hair, his cheeks flushed.

"Sorry," he says.

"It's okay. He seemed nice."

Parker chuckles. "He's a giant turd, but I love him."

We talk for a couple more minutes before saying goodbye, and I find that I miss him even more now. Though I did notice that Archer called me Parker's boyfriend and Parker didn't deny it, which felt really good. Does he consider me his boyfriend? We never really had that talk, just the "we're not sleeping with anyone else" talk. But I don't know if that's like a "we're dating" thing or a "friends with benefits but with exclusivity" kind of thing. And I guess there's still a part of me that doubts that Parker would want more than just sex with me, or friendship, even though I want everything with him.

The following day is Ava and Addison's martial arts graduation, and then shopping.

I text Jackson that evening because I'm still worried about him after what happened at the party.

Me: You okay? I'm worried about you. You don't have to tell me anything but I'm here if you need someone to talk to. He doesn't respond right away, which has been happening a lot more lately, but eventually my phone buzzes with a reply.

Jackson: Hey, babe. I know I've been acting weird lately, sorry. I honestly am not the best right now but I will be okay. I'm not ready to share yet, but I promise I will when I've figured things out more. Don't worry about me. Have a good Christmas. Love you Kissy face emoji.

Me: love you too

I hate how sad my best friend sounds, even over text, and wish there was something I could do, but I guess the only thing to do is make sure he knows I'm here when he's ready to talk.

The next day we spend at home, just relaxing, watching movies and playing games as a family.

The following day, Dad goes to an art gallery with me while the girls go to a movie. And the day after that we go skiing as a family.

On Christmas Eve we go sledding at a hill nearby and while I've been texting with Parker over the past couple of days and talked to him almost every night, it's not the same as having him here. I just know he would love this. He would love everything we've done. Oreo even came into my room once and laid down where the air mattress used to be, looking so sad I had tears sliding down my cheeks again. She climbed up on my bed after that, and I hugged her while I cried.

Christmas morning is beautiful. There's a fresh blanket of snow on the ground and the fireplace is roaring. Mom has made her amazing cinnamon rolls again. There's coffee and hot chocolate and the tree looks amazing with all the lights lit up. Of course looking at it makes me think of Parker again, and my chest squeezes painfully.

I get some art supplies, some clothes, some books, and the girls squeal when they open their presents from me. I got Addison a science kit and Ava a jewelry making kit.

I'm up in my room putting my gifts away when there's a knock on the door. I turn to see Dad standing there, a soft smile on his rugged face.

"Hey, can I come in?" he asks, and I nod. He sits on the bed and pats the spot next to him. It's been a while since Dad and I had a chat, but I'm very familiar with the gesture. He did the same thing when I came out at the age of twelve, and when I was being bullied in school. And when I was scared of learning to drive. And before I left for college.

Tears are already filling my eyes when I sit down next to him and I wipe them away.

"Listen, bud," he starts, his voice gentle as he grips my

shoulder and squeezes. "Your Mom and I wanted to see how you're doing. You've seemed sad since you got here and we want to make sure everything is okay."

"Yeah," I nod, wiping tears away again, but more keep coming. "Yeah, I'm fine."

He gives me a rueful smile and I flush. "It's okay if you're not fine. It's okay if you miss him, son."

I start to sob then and bury my face in Dad's shoulder as he wraps his arm around me. "I shouldn't miss him this much," I sniffle. "It's only been a few days, and I'm with you guys."

He chuckles and his shoulder moves against me. "Love doesn't work that way, bud."

I raise my head and stare at him. I swallow. "I don't–" He levels me with a look that says he wasn't born yesterday and I flush again.

"Wanna try that again?" he says, his voice a mixture of compassion and humor.

"Shit," I say, more tears sliding down my cheeks as I bury my face in Dad's shoulder again. "I'm in love with him."

"I know," he says, rubbing my back.

"I'm sorry I've been so miserable. I don't mean to be rude. I really am enjoying being home."

"I know that, too," he says. "And we're glad to have you here. But we need you to leave."

"What?" I say, raising my head again, eyes wide.

He laughs and grips the back of my neck. "You need to see him, Rory. And if you're feeling brave enough, you need to tell him how you feel."

"But I don't go back to school for a week," I point out.

"I know, but your Mom and I were thinking that maybe you'd like to fly out to see Parker over break."

My eyes widen even further. "What?"

"We want you to be happy, Rory. And we know you love us, but we also knew that at some point you would meet someone who would be the man you deserved and that he would come first."

"But, Ava and Addison–"

"Will be fine. They are perceptive, too, and they love you. I think if you don't get on a plane and tell that boy how you feel, they might not let you join their tea parties anymore." He grins and so do I.

———

Twenty four hours later, I'm climbing out of the Uber that dropped me off in front of what I'm hoping is Parker's house, or this is going to be hella awkward. I didn't tell him I was coming. I kinda wanted to surprise him, or maybe I am still trying to screw up the courage to tell him how I feel, but I'm telling myself it's the former, or I might pass out. My parents said they talked with Parker's parents, so I'm not surprising everyone.

The weather is beautiful. It's mid afternoon in California, sunny, warm, and just about perfect with the breeze ruffling my hair as I take a deep breath and knock on the front door.

I hear voices inside and can't help laughing when someone, not Parker, says, "Because I told you to, dick face, and I'm older. Move it."

The door opens and Parker is standing there mumbling, "That doesn't even make any sense," when he sees me. His eyes widen and his mouth gapes.

"Little rabbit?" he says, and my chest squeezes.

"Hi."

The next thing I know he's got his arms around me and my feet are off the ground as he squeezes me so tightly I think I feel a couple of ribs cracking. I wrap my legs around him and hold on as his grip on me loosens enough for me to breathe again. Then we're staring at each other, and I can't believe how fucking happy I am.

"Is it really you?" he says, and I nod.

"I can't believe you're here. God, I've missed you so much. I–" he stops short and swallows and I can't wait any longer.

"I love you," I blurt. Then my nerves catch up with me when he just stares and I word vomit. "I hope that's not super awkward when we're not even technically dating, or maybe we are, but I don't know for sure. We've never actually been on a date, unless you count those parties at school, and I don't really count that, but if you want to that's fine. And if you don't feel the same, that's fine, too. I don't want to pressure you. And now I'm realizing maybe I should stop talking but I'm super scared that if I stop you'll tell me something I don't want to hear so I'm just gonna keep going until–"

His lips crash against mine and I grunt as he kisses me hard, holding me tighter again. I tighten my legs around his waist and my arms around his neck, kissing him back.

"I love you, too," he says, when he pulls away. "God, little rabbit, I'm so fucking in love with you."

I can't stop smiling and he kisses me again. "And we are dating," he tells me when we've finally pulled back for air.

I giggle. "Okay."

"I would carry you inside but someone should get your suitcase," he says, and I let him set me down. He takes my luggage in one hand and my hand in the other and we step inside. "I'm afraid it's not the quietest environment. My family doesn't really do quiet, but we can go up to my room for some privacy. I should probably introduce you to everyone first, though. My sisters and Mom are at the movies, but you can meet Archer, Aaron and Dad."

I nod, clinging to his hand tightly.

"Hey, you gonna let us meet the boyfriend?!" someone hollers from further inside the house.

Parker flushes but grins at me, and tugs me past the entryway and down the hall. He stops at a large open living area and kitchen where three men sit watching ESPN. The man who I'm assuming is his dad sits in a leather recliner. He looks how I imagine Parker will in about thirty years. Tall, muscular, but with a bit of spare tire around his middle, and thick hair that's got more gray in it than brown. He's wearing glasses and a kind smile.

"Hey, there he is," he says, reaching his hand out for me to shake. "I'm Roger. We've heard a lot about you, Rory. It's nice to meet you." Out of the corner of my eye I see one of the twins throwing popcorn at the other, who is doing his best to ignore his brother.

"Thank you. It's nice to meet you, too. Thanks for letting me stay." The brother who is being attacked by the popcorn turns and gives the other brother a wet willie and that one shouts in protest before reaching over and tweaking the nipple of the other one. I'm so distracted by it all, but Parker and Roger aren't even looking at them, like they're completely used to this behavior, which I suppose they are.

"Of course. The more the merrier." He turns back to the tv like his sons aren't practically wrestling on the couch now, one with the other in a headlock.

Even though I've already sort of met Archer, I can't tell them apart to save my life.

"Say it," the one giving the headlock says.

"No," the other protests, and I look at Parker.

"Are they always like this?"

"Oh, this is nothing," he tells me. "This is them being calm."

I laugh and then laugh even more when the one giving the headlock repeats, "Say it."

"Dude, I'm not telling you you're prettier than me. We're fucking identical twins. Now get your hands off me."

Parker shakes his head but there's a smile on his face when he grips my waist and hauls me up again. I let out an "eep" but smile and cling to him like a koala as he carries me towards the stairs. "They could be at that for a while. You can meet them officially later."

"What about the suitcase?"

"It can wait," he tells me with a grin. He makes his way

up the stairs with relative ease, grinning at me more as we pass a bathroom and two more bedrooms on the way to his room. When we're finally inside, Parker shoves the door closed with his foot and tosses me on the bed.

I squeak in surprise as I land on the mattress and then smile widely as he climbs on and hovers over me. "I can't believe you're here," he says, his thumb brushing against my bottom lip and his hazel eyes fixed on mine. "God, I was going crazy missing you."

"Me, too," I say, and glance at his lips. His mouth meets mine and I groan into the kiss. It only takes a few seconds of his tongue tangling with mine and his fingers playing with my nipple through the fabric of my shirt before I'm rock hard and leaking into my panties.

"Jesus, little rabbit," he rasps, pulling away. "I can't get enough of you."

My response is a whimper as I pull him back to me, kissing him harder and bucking my hips up into him.

He moans, and I pull back this time. "Should we be doing this?" I ask, trying to catch my breath as my cock aches in my jeans. "With your family downstairs?"

"Yes," he says, then starts kissing my neck as he continues to play with my nipples. I moan and tilt my head back. "It's just my dad and brothers." More kisses. "They'll be fine. Not like they haven't fucked or jerked off with me in the house a billion times."

"What if..." my words come out slowly as I gasp and moan at the way he licks and bites at my neck. "What if they hear us? You know I'm not quiet."

"Oh, Aaron and Archer are standing outside the door listening to everything already."

"What?" I say, eyes wide. Parker stops his onslaught of my neck and grins at me.

"Are not!" a voice comes from the hall, and my eyes widen even further.

"For fuck's sake," another voice says, "I told you you were breathing too loud."

Parker rolls his eyes and I don't think I've ever actually seen him do that before. I can't help laughing.

"It wasn't my breathing, shit for brains," the first voice says. "It was your stench. God, when was the last time you bathed?"

"Come here, you have something in your eye."

"Ouch."

I'm laughing even more now, and trying not to, and Parker shouts, "Get away pervs, you're scaring Rory."

"Make it good for him, bro!" one of the twins shouts. I still can't tell which one.

Parker flushes and so do I, but we hear footsteps padding down the hall and a, "Oh my god, stop it. You're such a loser."

Parker shakes his head, but he's grinning again when he looks at me.

"I love you," I tell him, and his grin gets wider.

"I love you, too," he says, and kisses me again.

We make love, and forget Parker's family. I am almost certain that with how amazing Parker is making me feel, the entire neighborhood can hear me.

EPILOGUE

SIX YEARS LATER

RORY

"Papa!" my daughter shrieks, her chubby little toddler legs carrying her to the front door and her pigtails bouncing as Parker steps inside. He crouches and she jumps into his arms. Then he's spinning her around and showering her with kisses, making her squeal even more in delight.

I have our son on my hip as I reach my husband and press up on my tiptoes to kiss him. He beams at me and presses a kiss to Ethan's cheek.

The twins, Emily and Ethan, are two now. We married four years ago, shortly after graduation, and having children early on was never something Parker and I hesitated on. We both knew we wanted them, and growing our family has been wonderful in so many ways. It's had it's challenges, too, of course, but I always knew that whatever we faced we would do it together, and we have.

My noise sensitivity has been a struggle with young kids in the house, like we knew it would be, but I didn't want it to keep us from having them. I've managed with my ear plugs, and our next door neighbor, Ruth, is a super sweet lady in her sixties who lives alone and watches them a couple of days a week so I can get a break and get some work done. She's amazing with them and they adore her. She also loves Parker's cooking, just like everyone else, so we pay her in cupcakes and cookies and the occasional dinner, and since we live only a few short minutes from my parents and my sisters, who are now thirteen, we have lots of people willing to babysit for us.

We've had to be very selective about the toys we purchase and that we allow our families to purchase for the kids so it doesn't make things harder for me, and they've all been supportive and understanding of that, which I really appreciate.

I try to make sure we have enough quiet activities throughout the day so I can relax. We read, and paint, and color, and go for walks, usually stopping for a visit with Ruth along the way.

The best part of the day, though, is when Parker steps through the door. He is the best partner a guy could ask for, and he adores the kids. He just started his fourth year working at the local elementary school as the physical education teacher, and he does some personal training on the side. He's busy, but he loves his work and we're always so excited to see him at the end of the day.

I work from home, doing illustrations for children's books, a couple of which have been Amazon best sellers and helped me gain more traction and a large and steady following on social media. I also do artwork for authors who reach out wanting character art done for one of their stories and I enjoy it very much. The twins keep me busy, of course, but I get in as many hours as I can while they nap and at night after they've gone to bed, or on the days they're with Ruth.

We visit with Parker's family a couple of times a year, and while I wish we all lived within ten minutes of each other, we have time with them every Christmas and spend a good deal of our summers in California.

Our house is a mess like always, because we're busy little

bees and it's like they say, cleaning a house with a toddler in it is like brushing your teeth while eating Oreos. And with two toddlers it's nearly impossible. There's toys everywhere, and Peppa Pig playing on the TV when we make our way back into the living room.

Parker just grins at me as he surveys the mess and settles on the floor to play with the kids for a bit. I join him as we stack blocks, let the kids make a treat in their toy kitchen and rave about how amazing it is, and then read a story, before we let them entertain themselves while we make dinner. The open floor plan allows us to have a view of them while we cook, and I smell something that most definitely isn't dinner a moment later.

"I'll get it," Parker says, and moves to the living room to decipher who the culprit is. He pulls Ethan's pants back to check his diaper and then Emily. He wrinkles his nose and then scoops her up, hauling her over his shoulder to her bedroom and the changing station as she giggles and kicks her feet.

We eat dinner as a family, and then Parker tells me he'll clean up while I take a break. I hide in our bedroom upstairs and run a bath for myself, bubbles included. I stick my headphones on and listen to music as I relax and soak, knowing our children are safe and cared for by their Papa.

He is the best man I know, the love of my life, and I can't believe I get to spend the rest of my life with him. He proposed on my birthday our senior year, with all of our friends there celebrating, and I'm pretty sure my squeal of "yes" was heard all over campus.

Who would have thought that a horrible first encounter in a bathroom stall when I was just trying to find someone to help me get over a sleazy ex boyfriend, would lead to where we are now? I'm thankful everyday that my eyes were opened to how much better I deserved and that I found someone who loved me for exactly who I am, who encourages me, strengthens me, cares for me and loves me in a way that I hope our children one day experience with their partners, should they choose to have them.

After putting the twins to bed that night we curl up on the sofa to watch a movie, me in one of Parker's T-shirts and him in the sweats he still has from college. We're both exhausted, and I'm nodding off on his shoulder an hour later. He turns the tv off and scoops me up. I sigh contentedly as my head rests against his firm chest, and I feel us moving up the stairs.

I curl up on my side when he lays me in bed, and hum as his warm body presses against mine, his strong arm coming around to hold me close.

He presses a kiss to my ear. "Goodnight," he murmurs, his warm breath tickling my skin. "Love you, little rabbit."

I grin at his use of the nickname for me. "Love you, too." I grip his arm and pull it tighter around me as we drfit to sleep, feeling safe and loved and so very happy.

The End

Thank you for reading Parker and Rory's story. If you enjoyed it please consider leaving a review! They are a big help!

ABOUT THE AUTHOR

I live in sunny Florida with my husband and three children. I love reading and writing mm romance and am an advocate of mental health and chronic pain awareness. I love rainy days and sunshine and curling up with a good book or watching my favorite tv shows. I'm a big fan of the tv show Supernatural and believe that Starbucks is a form of self-care :)

You can follow me on social media, join my facebook group Felicity Snow's Followers, sign up for my newsletter, see my Pinterest storyboards, and find my other books here:

linktr.ee/felsnowauthor

www.ingramcontent.com/pod-product-compliance
Lightning Source LLC
LaVergne TN
LVHW090517110826
845146LV00003B/891

* 9 7 9 8 9 9 4 9 8 3 3 0 0 *